Bessie A. Turner

ALBERTYPE,

E. BIERSTADT, NEW YORK.

A WOMAN

IN THE CASE.

A Story.

By Miss Bessie A. Turner,
AUTHOR OF "CIRCUMSTANTIAL EVIDENCE."

"I do but beg a little changeling boy."—*Shakspeare.*

NEW YORK:
G. W. Carleton & Co., Publishers.
LONDON: LOW, SON & CO.
MDCCCLXXVI.

Copyright, 1875, by
G. W. CARLETON & CO

John F. Trow & Son,
PRINTERS AND STEREOTYPERS,
205–213 *East 12th St.*,
NEW YORK.

PREFACE.

SOME books are written to sell; others to illustrate a principle. I shall have attained both objects, if this little work meets with popular favor. I believe in individual freedom of writing and buying. I have written for my own pleasure and profit. If the public purchase for the same reasons, both parties will be satisfied. My story is founded on fact, but I think it will be conceded that it is "stranger than fiction." If curious people expect to find anything in it bearing directly or indirectly on the great "trial," in the elucidation of which I was necessarily made a witness, I am happy to know they will be disappointed. It may, however, be some consolation for them to learn that had it not been for that misfortune, it would be possible for me to earn an honest living in a less public way than this. As it is, I have chosen a path which I hope will lead to profit and favor.

B. T.

NEW YORK, *October*, 1875.

CONTENTS.

A WOMAN IN THE CASE.

CHAPTER I.

THE RUSSELLS.

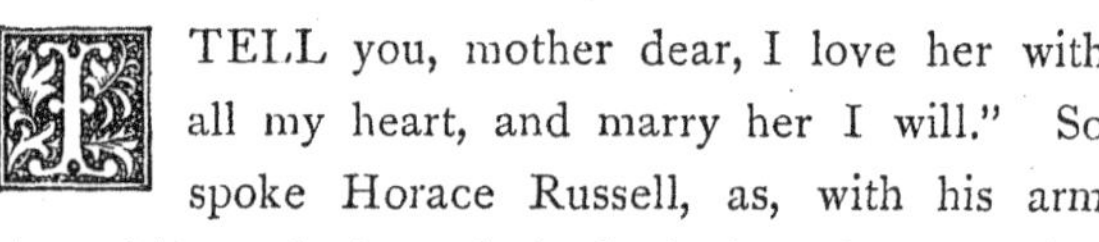

I TELL you, mother dear, I love her with all my heart, and marry her I will." So spoke Horace Russell, as, with his arm about his mother's neck, he looked at the retreating form of Jenny Marvin, his sweetheart and intended bride.

Born in a manufacturing village of England, and reared in the immense establishment of which his father was the founder and proprietor, Horace Russell was as fine a specimen of the better grade of the English middle class as one would care to see. He had barely turned his twenty-third year, stood six feet in his stockings, carried himself with the air of a hunter, and was noted, at all the fairs, as the best jumper wrestler, boater and marksman in the county. His early years had been spent in acquiring the ruder elements of education ; but his head was bent on mechanics, and his delight was to go to the factory, watch the machinery, learn of the men the why and the wherefore, and perfect himself in all that pertained to his father's affairs. At the age of eighteen, at the urgent request of Horace, Mr. Russell, senior, put him at work, and on his twenty-first birthday the young man was hailed as foreman of the works.

The Russell family was of humble origin, self respecting, frugal, and well-to-do. Joseph Russell came of virtuous stock, and looked upon merry-making as a sin. Nevertheless, he married young, and, at the period of which we write, was the contented husband of a devoted wife, and the happy father of two sons, Horace and Harry, the latter a cripple. In the factory and at home the will of Joseph Russell was law. The wife, as good a soul as ever breathed, trembled at the least exhibition of impatience by Horace, who had a high temper, and shrank with apprehension at every elevation of tone, lest it might be the beginning of an unknown end to be avoided and dreaded. Harry was a cripple from his birth ; he was intelligent, quick-witted, sagacious and kind. Books were his refuge, and study his delight. Between the tender-hearted mother, the sturdy Horace and the pale-featured Harry, were bonds of sympathy to which Joseph, who was *brusque* in manner and rude of speech, was an utter stranger.

And yet, Joseph loved his wife and loved his sons. Of Harry's proficiency at school he was very proud, and whatever the young man desired, was readily granted, at whatever cost; while in the tact and marvellous intuition of Horace, the honest manufacturer found not only pleasure but profit.

Twenty-three years had passed, and aside from the little misunderstandings incident to well-regulated families, nothing had happened to mar the home-harmony, or jar the sense of love till now; but now it had come. And this was it.

Jennie Marvin worked in the factory.

Pretty?

She was beautiful in the eyes of all who saw her, but to Horace she was the incarnation of all that is good and sweet, and true and pure. Her parents were very poor while living; so much so, that in sunshine and in rain, Jennie was compelled to walk daily to the factory, that the small wages she received might eke out the pittance gathered here and there by a willing but a shiftless father. Fever deprived Jennie of her father, and consumption, tantalizingly cruel in its grasp, threatened for months the life of the mother, upon whose blessings Jennie lingered long and wistfully after death had closed the poor woman's eyes, leaving the orphaned girl of eighteen to fight for bread as best she could.

A pretty picture was the dainty girl, as turning through the stile, dressed in modest garb, she blushingly acknowledged the foreman's kindly greeting, and hastily passed to her section. They had known each other from infancy, and with the crippled brother had sat upon the same forms, played the same pranks, suffered the same punishments, and shared each other's lunch. As years rolled along, the exactions of domestic drudgery kept Jennie at home, the studies of Harry required his attention at the academy, and Horace's love of his father's work sent him to the factory, so that save a glimpse now and then at church, an occasional meeting on the street, or, perchance, a dance at the county fair, the three rarely met. In the course of time, however, Jennie sought and obtained employment at the mill, and from that time on, her daily presence revealed to Horace the charms of head and heart which later led him to the step which eventually changed the course of his life, and brought about a collision from which he would willingly have shrunk.

Between Horace and Harry there were no secrets. The boys loved each other. In the heat of summer Horace protected Harry, and in the winter he shielded him from the blast. Whatever the one lacked in physical requirements, the other more than supplemented. Play and interplay was the habit of their lives. Horace rejoiced in Harry's successes at the academy, and when the elder disclosed in the secresy of their chamber an invention with which he hoped to surprise and profit their father, the delight of the one far eclipsed the hopefulness of the other. And between the boys and their mother, too, was a most delightful sympathy. To her they confided the troubles of their boyhood, to her they told the embarrassments of maturer years. She, mother-like, was full of consideration, of kindness, of sympathy. She concealed their faults, made peace with their father, aided and abetted them in all their schemes, and did as all good mothers do, oiled the machinery of home, so that there was but little friction and not a bit of flame.

And yet, although Horace had told his mother every trouble he had ever experienced, every annoyance of his life, every purpose and ambition of his heart, when he discovered his love for Jennie Marvin he said nothing to her—but told it all to Harry.

They both jumped to one conclusion.

They both knew the opposition to come from their father.

And when Horace said to Harry "if I can gain her consent to-night, I shall do it," they both felt it was the entering wedge of serious trouble in the family.

Now Joseph Russell was by no manner of means a bad hearted man. On the contrary he was as honest and true as steel. He paid his debts, went to church, had family prayers, spoke kindly of his neighbors, dealt generously with his people, and was reputed one of the most straightforward men in the county—but he had a weakness.

He wanted to leave his sons one grade higher on the social scale than he was himself.

Nothing that money could do was grudged in Harry's education.

Nothing that time and patience, and industry and zeal could accomplish, was withheld in his pursuit of wealth for the elevation of his son and heir.

In his eyes the marriage of his son with one of his factory hands would be a step backward, which the boys well knew he would never for a moment sanction.

Harry and his mother canvassed the matter time and time again while Horace and his father were at their work, but the way seemed darker the more they searched for light. Harry was fond of the girl; she had always been kind and considerate of him when they were children, and even if there were no other bond, the fact that Horace loved her, made Jennie sacred and loveable in his eyes. To his mother Harry recounted all the tender things Horace had told him about Jennie, and after much persuasion induced her to agree with him, that after all it was the happiness of Horace they were bound to consider, and further to pledge her influence with her husband, in favor of the union, or at all events the engagement. With a light heart Horace heard Harry's report one pleasant summer night, and he determined that not another day should pass before he disclosed his love to Jennie, and received by word of mouth her acceptance of his hand.

CHAPTER II.

A WOMAN IN THE CASE.

MR. Russell's great factory gave constant employment to three hundred men and women during the busy season, and by a system of gradation-payments furnished them all a comfortable living the entire year. Very naturally the master of so many people was the great man of the town, and his influence was acknowledged and sought by the neighboring gentry and magnates of the county. Always a self-willed and imperious man, Joseph Russell became in time little better than a conscientious tyrant, exacting from everyone a full measure of work, and giving with equal fairness a full measure of pay. At home he was never genial, but never morose. He was making money, his wife was anxious to please, and his children were reputable and industrious and obedient. He knew that Harry's infirmity would necessitate a life of ease, and for that he was prepared. To Horace he looked for aid in business, and after several years of trial concluded to make him a partner, establish him in a home, and gradually leave to him the entire management of his affairs. He talked freely with his wife of his plans, and announced to her that on Horace's next birthday he should hand to him the papers of partnership, give a grand holiday-party to the hands, and make his son in name, what he had been for some time in fact—the master of the mill.

The good mother was delighted and imparted an added zest to her husband's pleasure by accepting his plan as perfect, and endorsing his idea as the best that could be devised.

At breakfast Mr. Russell said: "Horace, will you drive over to town with me this morning? I have business with Mr. Wilson, the lawyer, which may need your counsel."

Horace, glad of an opportunity to tell his father of his love, cheerfully consented, and together they drove off, waving good-bye to the "housekeepers"—as they called Mrs. Russell and Harry—as they stood together on the broad stone in front of their pleasant home.

The father was full of his project, and he meant to broach it that morning.

The son was full of his love, and he meant to tell it then and there.

"Horace," said Mr. Russell, "you have been in the factory a long time, and are the best foreman I ever had. That's good. I'm glad of it, for I should hate to have my son behind the rest. Your mother and I have been talking the matter over, and I have concluded to take you into the business, half-and-half—now don't speak—so that you can have your hand on the crank if anything should happen to me. And that's what I'm taking you over to town for."

For a moment Horace looked at his father in blank astonishment. If an angel from Heaven had promised him the desire of his heart, he wouldn't have been more delighted and surprised. Tears filled his eyes, and the warm blood flushed his cheeks, as he grasped his happy father by the hand, and thanked him with an iron grip which meant much more than words.

Then in a moment he said: "Whatever you say, father, I will do, and thank you."

"Well, well, that's all settled then," said Mr. Russell. "And now, Horace, you must get a wife—get a good wife. Get a wife like your mother, my boy, and life will be easier. Look at me. Look at home—everything bright as a guinea and round as a ball. By the way, Horace, our Member was saying the other day that he would be pleased to have us call at his place. He has a fine family—two beautiful girls. Who knows what might happen, eh? But—bless me; what's the matter with the boy? Why don't you speak? I believe—but no, nonsense, that's absurd; Horace, what are you thinking of?"

"Well, father, there's no use in my trying to keep secret what must come out. I had determined to tell you all about it, anyhow, to-day. I was thinking of the dearest girl on earth, father. You know her, you like her. So does mother, so does Harry. I wanted to tell you that although nothing final has passed between us, I am in love with Jennie Marvin; and with your permission mean to make her my wife."

If Horace had knocked his father out of the wagon he could not have shocked him more.

Had he lost his senses? No, the bay team were making ten miles an hour over a lovely English road, the sunlight was dancing through the trees and across the meadow, the reins were in his hands, and Horace sat by his side, sturdy as an oak and gentle as a child.

"Conscience guide me!" said Mr. Russell, and then turning to his son, broke out in a perfect torrent of expostulation, censure, abuse and invective, until fairly white with rage he said: "Next Monday will be your birthday. I give you till then to decide. Forget this girl, strike hands with your father, and be a man. Adhere to her, and I disinherit you, turn you off,—and don't you dare to darken my door again. You know me. Now no more about it."

"But, father," began Horace——

"I tell you no more about it," rejoined his father. "Here we are at the post-office; mail this letter, order these books for Harry, and let's get back as soon as we can. We won't see Mr. Wilson to-day, I'm in no mood for business."

Horace did as he was bid; and together they drove homeward, unhappy, discontented, and utterly uncongenial.

As they entered the drive-way, Mrs. Russell met them near the gate, and in a moment saw that there was trouble between them.

"Why, what's the matter, father?" said she.

"Ask Horace," was his reply; and without another word to either of them he turned his back and strode off to the mill.

As he did so, the sweet face of Jennie Marvin peeied out from a group of nurslings by the hedge, and a soft voice said: "Good morning, Mrs. Russell; good morning, Horace." There she was, the cause of the first serious misunderstanding between father and son; the simple-hearted, blue-eyed beauty for whom Horace would give his life with pleasure.

"Why, how late you are, Jennie," said Horace.

"Yes, I know it, Horace; but I was kept at widow Harden's until after eight; she is very low, and I promised the Doctor I would care for her till some of the other neighbors looked in. But I'm all right now, only I thought I'd give you a surprise, and catch you making love to your mother. Good-bye," said Jennie, and off she went to her work.

"And that's the girl you love is it, Horace?" said Mrs. Russell.

"Indeed it is," said he, "and I tell you, mother dear, I love her with all my heart; and marry her I will."

He then told his mother all his father had said, and, after begging her to intercede with her husband, said: "If the worst comes, mother dear, I have £200 of my own. We are both young and strong. I'll marry Jennie at once, and together we'll fight our way through life, bringing no discredit on the name, and perhaps be able sometime to repay the love and kindness you have always shown me. So, mother, dry your eyes; help me if you can—and if not, I'll help myself."

CHAPTER III.

HE ASKS : SHE ANSWERS.

NOT a word was exchanged between Horace and his father all day. After tea, at night, the young man, who was as frank and honest in heart as he was noble and truthful in appearance, laid his hand upon his father's shoulder, and giving it a loving grip, said : "Father, I am going down to see Jennie. Let me take a kind word from you ?"

It was well meant, but the boy did not understand the man.

Without changing his position, Joseph Russell said : "You know my wish—obey it, and all's well ; thwart it. and we are no more to each other forever."

Mrs. Russell said nothing, though she looked unutterable sympathy ; but Harry, who loved his father, mother, and brother as one, rose hastily from the table, and throwing himself full upon his father's breast, begged and implored him to be considerate, to wait, to hear what Horace proposed, and at all events to withdraw what seemed, to an over-sensitive nature, very much like a curse.

But it was useless.

A stubborn man is harder to move than a mule, and Joseph Russell was precisely that.

The end of it all was that the father pretended to read the county paper, his wife busied herself with tearful eyes about her domestic duties, Harry wept alone, full length upon his bed, and Horace went to see his love.

Of course he went.

He had told Jennie that afternoon, as she was leaving the mill, that he should see her in the evening, and as he had something to say to her, should wish her to take a walk with him by the side of the river.

Quick as a flash Jennie saw, or rather felt—for women always feel situations long before they are apparent to men,—that something had gone wrong; but wisely saying nothing, she quickly put on her hat, and together they passed into the street.

Ordinarily, Horace was tired with his day's work, and inclined to rest. He didn't object to being talked to, but he hated to answer questions. He was like a vast majority of the better grade of men who like the attentions and loving ways of women, but do not encourage inquisitiveness, even if it be born of genuine interest.

But on this occasion every nerve was alert, and every fibre on a quiver. He hurried Jennie along at a pace very much faster than a lover's lounge, until they reached the bank of a beautiful stream, protected by superb old trees, through whose leaves the bright beams of an August moon gleamed and glistened.

Taking her head in his two hands, he turned up to the full gaze of his impassioned eyes, and the full light of the curious moon, one of the sweetest of faces.

He didn't stop to kiss her.

Without a caress, without premonition of any kind, he spoke to her, and in such earnestness that she felt the gravity and sincerity of every word.

"I know you love me, Jennie. You have told me so a thousand times and more. You love me devotedly, and I—well, I love you well enough to make you my wife, and that's about as much as man can do. I leave my father. I go at once. I have £200 in cash, my head, my hands, and a constitution of iron. I want from you an answer now; will you be my wife, will you join me hand to hand and go with me in search of home and fortune? Say yes. Don't mar it by a but, or an if, or a why. If you love me, say yes. Will you?"

Throwing her arms about his neck, and burying her face in the bosom of her lover, Jennie answered as he wished; but how, or in what language, is not given us to tell.

The passion was over, and after the natural interchange of vows, assurances, and asseverations customary at such times, Horace told Jennie the whole story, and anticipated her objections and demurrals, by saying that he had written to Liverpool for information respecting the steamers, and that doubtless the whole affair, separation, marriage, and embarkation for New York, to which point he had concluded to go, would be consummated by the close of the following week.

"And yet," said he, "I shall hate to leave mother, it will almost kill Harry, and how father and the mill will get on without me, is more than I can tell."

But with an effort, he pushed away all the unpleasant features, turned to Jennie, his betrothed, kissed her again and again, and after leaving her at her door, started homeward at a rapid gait.

At the gate he met his mother. "Why, mother, it's after ten o'clock; what are you doing here?"

"Waiting for you, darling," said she; "waiting for my first-born son. Can you not give up this love, dear Horace?"

"Mother——"

"But hear me, darling. Can you not wait?"

"Mother, I love Jennie. She has promised to be my wife, and before a week is passed marry her I will."

"Heaven bless you, my son. Heaven bless you. Come what may your mother loves you, trusts you, and will always pray for you and yours. Good-night, my boy. Remember he is your father. Speak gently. It will do no harm, for he loves you very much and his disappointment is very great."

They parted affectionately, as their custom was, and long hours passed before Horace reached his room, and throwing his arm over his beloved Harry, fell into a deep and restful sleep.

CHAPTER IV.

TEN YEARS LATER. A SUMMONS.

TEN long years of hard work, disappointment, domestic comfort, bereavement, hope, anxiety and struggle passed over the heads of Horace Russell and his faithful wife. They had crossed the ocean, found a home in Michigan, buried a daughter, made a fortune, lost it in a fire, and grown mature in each others respect and love.

Occasional letters from home had told of the gradual decline and death of the gentle mother; of the sudden paralysis and death of the loving Harry; of the princely wealth and hardening character of the father, and such lighter gossip as brings one's childhood's home and days so vividly before the absent.

With a few thousand dollars laid away for a rainy day, Horace felt that he was comfortable, but not content. His mind was active, but the necessity of daily occupation left him but little leisure for study in his peculiar line. He knew that he had material in his mind, which if utilized, would make him rich and perhaps famous. But like Mary of old he hid all these things in his heart, and never by look or word gave hint to Jennie of the unrest which was a canker to his life.

On the 16th of August 1854 he received a letter postmarked London.

The handwriting was unfamiliar, and with some apprehension he opened it.

THE LETTER.

LONDON, *August* 2d, 1854.

DEAR SIR,—A message from my old friend, the Rev. Mr. Marsh, received this morning, tells me that your dear father has not long to live. When I occupied temporarily Mr. Marsh's pulpit, I had occasion to see much of Mr. Russell, and one evening he unburdened to me the secret of his life. He loves you. He longs once more to see you. And yet so stubborn was his pride, that he would not consent even that a message might be sent to you. Knowing as I do his critical condition, aware as I am of his fatherly affection for the boy of his early manhood, the first-born of his love, I have taken this liberty in your common interest, and beg you to lay aside whatever your occupation may be, and come here that you may receive your father's blessing, and I greatly fear to close your father's eyes.

Pardon me, if in sending you the enclosed Bill for

£100 I offend, but not knowing your circumstances, I take the same liberty with you, that I would wish taken with my son, if his father were dying, and he an exile.

With best wishes for your health, and earnestly begging you to come home at once,

I am, yours most truly,

JOHN HALL,

Rector of St. John's.

To HORACE RUSSELL, *Milwaukee.*

Enclosed, Bill on Brown Bro's & Co. for £100.

Jennie's round fair arm was encircling her husband's neck, and the little fat hands of Harry, their boy, were tearing the envelope at his feet.

For a moment the tears refused to come, but only for a moment. Then rising to his feet, the noble fellow said: "Jennie, love, see to the traps. I'll go down to the agent's—learn about the steamers, and be back in half an hour. For dearest, he is my father after all, you know; and if he had known you darling, as Heaven grant he may even yet, we never should have left him."

And off he went.

Of course the £100 were not needed.

The next day Horace drew his money, paid his bills, placed his affairs in the hands of a lawyer, packed up, and started for New York.

One week later he stood upon the deck of a superb Cunarder—but he stood alone, crying like a babe.

CHAPTER V.

THE BOY, OH WHERE WAS HE?

PERHAPS you think men should never cry.

Well, let us see.

Three days before this, Horace, his wife, and little Harry reached the Astor House, and were shown one of the best rooms in the hotel.

The next day was spent in necessary preparations for the voyage.

The day preceding the day of sailing was equally occupied until about six o'clock, when Jennie, being utterly exhausted, threw herself on the bed to rest.

Horace was weary, too.

But little Harry was cross.

Of course he was.

Two long days he had been left in the care of a chambermaid, who was kind and careless. He rolled a hoople through the halls till a call-boy stole it. He slid down the banisters until one of the guests complained at the office. He went into the dining-hall twenty times a day, and gorged himself until he was sick. He played marbles with a little boy from Boston, and won all his stock.

He wore himself out in the endeavor to amuse himself.

And when his father carried him up-stairs on his back, after dinner on Friday evening, he begged him to take him out for a walk.

Little Harry was five years old, tall of his age, smart, bright, quick, and full of fun. His hair was jet black, like his father's; his eye was a blue gray, like his mother's. Nothing frightened him, but he could be easily moved by his sympathies.

Altogether he was a loving, lovable boy—one of the kind that fathers whip and mothers shield; who always turn out well in spite of the lash, and develop qualities precisely the opposite to those which their "teachers and guardians" predict for their manhood.

However, out they went. The father proud of the son; the boy pleased with his father.

They walked over to the City Hall Park, and admired the architectural wonders of the building with its marble front and freestone rear. They wandered over the green grass, watched a free fight between two rival fire companies at the corner of Chatham and Frankfort streets, bought a penny glass of ice cream of an old woman near the Park, and were turning down-town towards the Astor House, when—

"Hallo! where's the boy?"

Quite a question, wasn't it?

Horace looked in vain.

He met one of Matsell's watchmen in an old-fashioned police hat, and told him his story.

Of course he wasted time.

What should he do?

The unfeeling crowd hurried by him. Carts and wagons and stages passed in everlasting procession along the street.

But the boy, the apple of his eye, the core of his heart, the darling of his wife—his wife! How should he tell his wife?

What should he tell his wife?

Half crazed with fear, full of bitter self-reproaches, uncertain which way to go, unfamiliar with the city and its ways, the poor fellow grasped the first man he could, and asked him to show him to the station.

Thinking Russell was drunk, the man shoved him off, and hurried on.

He spoke to another and was directed to the Chief's office, where all the satisfaction he could get was the tantalizing reply that if the boy turned up, the office would keep him until his father called.

"But I leave the country to-morrow," said Horace; "the steamer sails at nine, and we must be on board by eight."

"Oh, wait over," replied the Sergeant.

"My father is dying and I *must* go," rejoined Russell."

But of course "talk" did no good.

The officer took little Harry's name and description in his Book, thus :—

THE RECORD.

Person—Small boy.

Name—Harry Russell.

Age—Five years.

Description—Tall, slender.

Remarks—Lost near lower end of the City Hall Park. Horace Russell at Astor House.

"There, sir," said the "Sergeant, that's all right. You go home, and if the boy is found we'll take care of him. Now *don't* make a fuss. Good night." And with that he slammed the book upon the desk, by way of emphasis, and turned to read his paper.

Horace moved off with a heavy heart and hesitated long before he gave up the search, and went to tell his wife.

What words are adequate to picture that scene?

The heart-crushed man and the horror-struck woman looked at each other, as shrouded in despair, they saw their utter helplessness, and felt their desolation.

If Harry had died, they would have known the extent of their loss; but the very uncertainty of his fate added to their misery and gave poignancy to the sickness of their hearts.

Those of you who have laid your hearts in the grave can understand, partially, the feeling with which Jennie sat at the window through the weary hours of that long night, while Horace paced the streets.

You who have not known Death, need not seek to understand.

CHAPTER VI.

SHORT AND BITTER.

A MORNING of anguish ensued upon a night of frantic grief.

Horace felt the urgency of the errand he was on, and when the Police suggested that if he *must* go, possibly his wife could remain and prosecute the search, he accepted the proposition, and at once broached it to Jennie.

Well—she was a woman and a wife and a mother, and that tells the story. He went on, and she stayed behind.

She drove to the dock and watched the steamer; waving her handkerchief to her husband, as he stood leaning against the rail.

What wonder that the strong man wept?

CHAPTER VII.

LOVE MELTETH EVEN PRIDE.

H, the long, long days at sea!

And the nights—would they never end?

His heart was with his wife and boy, but his duty sternly beckoned Horace to his father's home.

Not an hour passed in the dreary day without its prayer to Heaven, that little Harry might be saved.

And in the weary watches of the night, the father heard the little fellow's cry, and starting, found he heard it not.

The Captain and some of the passengers knew of the circumstances attending Horace's trip, and endeavored to console him by such suggestions as naturally occur to men of the world; but the heart-sick parent heeded them not. And even while he looked ahead to the meeting with his father, his very soul lingered longingly near the dear ones in New York.

Every storm brought pictures of Harry's distress

before his eyes; and when the full features of the August moon disclosed themselves in the placid sky, wonder and imagination were busy with the possibilities of accident or harm to the wanderer.

At length Liverpool was reached, the kind Rector seen and repaid, the brisk drive made to the county town, near which were his father's works, and finally the mill itself loomed up beyond the stream, quickly followed by the house where he was born, and where his dear ones died.

Horace had left his home a youth, full of hope and courage.

He returned a man, sick in heart, anxious, restless, worn with care.

A strange face greeted him at the door. Entering he met the Doctor and a neighbor, to whom his coming was like the appearance of a welcome ghost, for not an hour in all the days went by in which the sick man did not murmur, "Horace, Harry, Horace Horace."

In a sentence, the condition of Joseph Russell was disclosed. It was possible, the Doctor said, that he might rally, and recover his senses before morning, but his death was a question of brief time only, and might indeed occur at any moment.

Hastily passing his friends, Horace made his way to the well-remembered bedroom.

On the wall hung the portrait of his blessed mother

There was the chair in which she sat and read to him on Sunday. The old-fashioned bureau standing in the corner still held the sampler she worked at school, and in a frame at the end stood a silhouette of her mother, cut by an artist at the County Fair. The brass hand-irons and the wooden stool were as natural as life, and the high-posted bedstead—

On that was his father.

His father indeed, but not the father of his thoughts.

He remembered a strong, athletic man; he saw a faded, dying paralytic.

Advancing cautiously to the side of the bed, Horace laid one hand gently on his father's ample brow, and pressing with the other the attenuated fingers which nervously played with the outer covering, whispered: "Father, I am Horace, do you know me?"

For a moment all was still.

The sick man opened his eyes.

His parched lips wanted water, and after it was given him, with an effort he partly raised himself in bed and began to speak, when he fell exhausted on the pillow.

Almost distracted, Horace called the doctor, who knew he was of no use, but very kindly came in, looked solemn, suggested the wetting of the lips, advised perfect quiet, and went out.

Presently Joseph Russell opened his great black

eyes again, smiled, sat up in bed, threw his arms upon his son, murmured: "Horace, Harry, Mary," and gave up the ghost.

For an instant Jennie and little Harry were blotted from existence.

For an instant boyhood resumed its being, and Horace was a romping lad, cheered on by Harry, laughed at by his mother, and chided by his prouder father.

And then—well, it only lasted an instant. Then he was a man again, with a father dead before him, a sorrowing wife he knew not where, and a boy—oh, what would Horace not have given if he could regain that boy?

After the funeral services, which were largely at tended by all the county some three days after, Mr. Wilson who had been Joseph Russell's man of business in all matters affecting law and formula, begged the favor of Horace's presence in the library.

He went.

"Mr. Russell," said Mr. Wilson, "as the sole heir and legatee of Joseph Russell, deceased, I have invited you here to take formal cognizance of the will of the decedent. He was a queer man, sir, a queer man. Would you believe it, sir, I never have read this will. He wrote it himself, sir, six years ago, the very night poor Harry died, when he tore up one I did write, and about which I of course knew everything. The will has been in my box six years, handed me by Joseph Russell himself, witnessed by me and my clerk, and we will read it sir, together.

THE WILL.

In the name of God, Amen. I, Joseph Russell, of Lewes, County Sussex, England, being in clear head and sound body, make this my will and testament, all others being destroyed and of no avail. My wife Mary is dead, God bless her. My son Harry is dead, God bless him. And I have no other kindred, heirs, or assigns."

Up to this point Mr. Wilson had read quite glibly; now he began to be apprehensive. Horace sat like a stone.

Mr. Wilson continued :—" My oldest son Horace Russell, God bless him, left his home years ago. I threatened to disinherit him. I never did, I never shall. He is bone of my bone, and flesh of my flesh. He has my pardon—I hope for his. To him, Horace Russell, I leave my house, my mills, my real estate, and all my property, real and personal, of whatever nature, to do with as he may elect, reserving such sums as he may find necessary for the discharge of my funeral expenses and other debts; and excepting £50 to each foreman, £2 to each operative, £500 to the parish of St. Sarah, and £10 per annum for the care of the ground where rest the dear bodies of Mary my wife, and Harry my son. Written with my own hand on one sheet of white foolscap paper, this 11th of August, 1849, and signed by me, and witnessed by John Wilson and Henry Place.

JOSEPH RUSSELL, L. S.

Witness,

JOHN WILSON, L. S.
HENRY PLACE, L. S.

"Gracious heavens, Mr. Russell!" said the gratified attorney, "this is handsome. Why, sir, you've a plum at least, sir. The mills themselves are worth three quarters of that, and you may rely on my calculation. I congratulate you, sir. When shall we go on?"

Horace never said a word.

In a moment £100,000 were placed at his disposal, and he never said one word.

Mr. Wilson began to feel out of place. Presently he was convinced that he had better retire.

Then he laid his card on the table, took his hat in his hand, and quietly stole away.

And Horace sat motionless for hours, and never said one word aloud.

CHAPTER VIII.

TILL DEATH DOTH THEM PART.

HORACE met his wife at the wharf.

Not a word was needed.

Her looks answered his distressed and anxious eye.

She had come home without the boy.

That night they slept in the old house, the dear old home where Horace was born, every room of which had its precious memory of those who were gone.

Slept did we say—far from it.

Held tightly in her loving husband's arms, Jennie told the ten days' story of her terrible experiences; how she had wearied the police with her importunity; how the Astor House people had kindly interested themselves in her trouble, and laid it before the chief magistrate of the city; how the press had aided her; and how after ten days of ceaseless energy, tireless activity and most faithful inquiry, they and she had been forced to see the utter uselessness of further search.

"And then, darling," said Jennie as floods of tears relieved her tired head, "I turned to you. I turned to you and longed to have you tell me where to look for comfort; how to reconcile my sorrow with my faith; how I could pray to a loving Saviour, with the grieving voice of Harry calling 'mamma' in my ears."

What could the strong man say?

How could he, whose very heart was dried to dust in grief, find waters of consolation for the crushed and broken woman at his side?

And so the night rolled on, beguiled by Horace's report concerning his father's death, his will, his business cares and sudden responsibilities, until as the early morning came they dropped to sleep.

To sleep, but not to rest.

Not to rest, for every noise startled Jennie from her slumber, and every movement of her husband brought her back to grief, and in every breath she dreamed of Harry, till, with the bright sunlight streaming in the window, she woke to repeat her experience, and Horace more exhausted than before, found nothing in his heart to say.

There are griefs and griefs, just as there are different kinds of people.

Some wear off; others wear in.

Horace felt quite as deeply as Jennie did, but upon him was laid *her* care, her comfort, and, perhaps he found in that duty a certain relief to which she was a stranger. And then he was at once so thoroughly immersed in business care that for many hours every day his mind was forced into other channels, and thus he was comforted.

But Jennie had no cares.

Her housekeeper took care of the establishment. She had no little ones to look out for. She found very little pleasure in renewing acquaintance with the few who remembered her as "that factory-girl who run off with Horace Russell," and she was literally left to self-communion and self-torture the greater part of the time.

She had authorized the police to pay one thousand dollars to any person who would give provable information about Harry, dead or alive, and she communicated regularly, through Mr. Wilson, with the New York authorities. At the end of a few months the lost boy had become a very old story to the officials, and finally the Chief wrote to Mr. Wilson that further correspondence was unnecessary, but that if anything was discovered at any time he would, of course, and at once, communicate with him.

From that date Jennie declined.

She declined fast.

Horace watched her like a lover, and tended her like a mother. Her slightest wish was a command. All her bodily wants were anticipated by the kindest of husbands, and assuming a cheer he was far from feeling, the generous fellow often endeavored to lead her into such pleasant paths of social excitement as were open to them.

But he failed.

His heart wasn't there,—and what excitement can take the place of interest?

Slowly, but surely, her decline developed into the foreshade of Death, and one bright moonlight night, with her feeble arms around her husband's neck, as his encircled hers, she sweetly smiled her crushed and broken heart into the eternal silence of an early grave.

CHAPTER IX.

TWENTY YEARS AFTER.

HE grave and reverend Matsell, superintendent of the New York police force, sat in his cosy inner office, dividing his precious time between the demolishment of a huge bunch of grapes and the mastery of a copy of formal "charges" preferred against the Board of Commissioners, when a formidable looking document, bearing the impress of the City's seal, was handed him.

Naturally cautious and careful of his digestion, he first finished his grapes and then broke the seal. In the envelope was the following

LETTER FROM THE MAYOR.

MAYOR'S OFFICE, NEW YORK, *August* 10, 1874.

SIR,—You will on receipt of this, detail a reliable and efficient officer from the Detective Bureau to aid Horace Russell, Esq., in a matter of importance. Mr. Russell can be found at the Clarendon Hotel to-morrow morning at nine o'clock, at which time let the officer report to him, and place himself absolutely at his disposal, until such time as his services are of no further use. Mr. Russell will provide whatever funds may be necessary in the undertaking, and the officer will be relieved of all other duty, until dismissed by him.

By order of the Mayor.

GEORGE C. KING, *Chief Clerk.*

To GEO. W. MATSELL, *Supt. Police.*

"Heaven bless me," said the old Chief. "What can this be? In the whole course of my official life I never have read such an order as this before. However, I'll soon know all about it."

Summoning Captain Irving, he asked which of the detectives would be most likely to serve the purpose desired. Without a moment's hesitation, Captain Irving replied:

"John Hardy, the keenest man I have, but I don't care to spare him for any length of time."

"Never mind that," rejoined the Chief, "send him to me."

In a few moments Officer John Hardy presented himself at the Superintendent's desk. Standing erect in the presence of his superior he was as handsome a man as one would see in a long day's walk. Apparently about twenty-four years old he was at least five feet ten inches high, straight and slender; his hair was jet black; his eyes an indescribable gray, looking blue or black as they were enlivened by humor or anger; his nose was not purely Grecian, but passed for such; and over a well formed lip, firm though full, hung a soft and graceful moustache. John had fun in him. Quick to detect the grotesque, easy tempered, with a sunny disposition, nervous, industrious and persevering, he had worked his way from the humble post of messenger, through every grade in the service, until he stood high in the esteem of his superiors as a detective of rare sagacity, wonderful intuition, and fairly magical in "luck."

All men have histories, but very few can look back upon a more eventful career—in humble life—than John Hardy.

His parents were scavengers. That is, his father was, and his mother—well she was a scavenger's wife, with the same skeleton and general formation as the rest of her sex: with love for her child like other women, and full of the ambitions, cares and anxieties common to us all.

John Hardy's father was a scavenger. That is, he used to go out in the morning with a bag, or basket, and a pick or rake, searching for what he might find. And he found a great deal. He found so much in gutter and street, in mound and filth, in sewer and refuse, that when he died his wife and son were heirs to

$5,000 and a tenement house worth $10,000 more, with a rental of $600 per annum.

The secrets of New York sewers are not open to the world. Even the keen eyes of New York reporters have not searched them out, and what reporters have not discovered must be tolerably well hid. Down in the dirty depths so black and full of gloom, myriads of nasty creatures hunt each other. Rats and slimy creeping things prey on weaker evidences of Nature's omnipresence. Water and slime slush through the channels; all manner of refuse finds its way to the outlet; jewels, the lost of every name, sink to the bottom, or lodge on the jutting stones; in other words under our streets, there are other avenues where life conceals itself, where riches pass side by side with the offscourings of the earth, and where the lantern of the scavenger discloses much that is terrible and sickening, but much, also, that is valuable and worth preserving.

A life spent in unveiling the mysteries of sewerage is not likely to be rich in anything, lest it be in the discovered wealth to be found in the dirt and muck of the streets; but scavengers are men, and there is no reason why they should necessarily be bad men.

At all events, John Hardy's father was so good a man as this: He loved his wife, and idolized their son.

He knew nothing of books, cared nothing for newspapers, and never went to church. But he sent John to school, and when the little fellow marched to the head of his classes, developing talent in every line of study, and, finally, stood before an audience of a thousand strangers, wearing the medals of honor, as he spoke the valedictory of his class, who shall say that the tears which coursed down the old man's cheeks were not as manly and as creditable to the scavenger, as though they were born of a philosopher or a student?

The Hardys' humble home was quite near Police Head-quarters, and long before John had left the public school he was as intimate and familiar there as any of the officers.

He was a bright boy, quick as a flash, and always ready to do errands for the *habitués* of the place.

When he left school he was made messenger in the Inspector's office, then a clerk, and after a subsequent term as roundsman, was detailed to detective duty, where we have found him.

"Officer Hardy," said the Superintendent, "I have received an order from the Mayor directing me to detail a prudent man from your bureau for an important duty. The Captain recommends you, and I confirm his selection. You will call on Mr. Russell, at the Clarendon, at 9 o'clock to-morrow morning, and place yourself at his disposal. I have no information as to his desires. Do whatever he directs, and in case of doubt report at once to me; you are relieved from duty here until further orders. Now do your best, Hardy. I have a feeling that this is to be a great opportunity. Why, I'm sure I don't know: but I do. That's all," and as Hardy went away the Chief reread the order from the Mayor, and wondered what it could refer to.

CHAPTER X.

HE AND SHE.

T nine o'clock on the following day officer Hardy, in citizen's dress, was ushered into the presence of Mr. Russell.

It was Horace.

Time had told upon him.

His head was bald as a billiard ball, and the locks which fringed the scalp and hung curling over the ears were gray. His eye was as bright as in the olden time, but his form was bent, and the close-shut mouth marked the firmness of his will, which had developed of late much like his father's.

Advancing to meet the detective, Mr. Russell looked at him with undisguised interest.

He expected to see a cast-iron soldier, straight, stiff and pompous.

In place of such a one he was confronted by an individual who might as well be taken for a gentleman of leisure as a man whose life was devoted to the unearthing of villany.

"Mr. Hardy, you are the officer I was told to expect this morning, I presume, and I am very glad to see you," said Horace Russell; "this is my wife and this my daughter."

At the moment of speaking two ladies entered the room, the elder a woman of perhaps forty years, a matron grave, dignified and handsome; the other a *petite* young miss, upon whose fair head some eighteen summers had cast their loving sunshine, leaving the golden impress on every waving tress.

"Take seats, please," said Mr. Russell; "I have much to tell Mr. Hardy, and he needs to be attentive."

"You would much better let mamma tell him, papa dear," said Maud, as she put a lump of sugar between the bars of her canary's cage. "She knows all about it, and you say yourself she is just as much interested in poor dear Harry as you are, and as for me, I'm fairly wild about him. Come, Mr. Hardy, you sit there near the window. Papa can have the easy-chair. I'll sit on this hassock by papa's knee; and mamma, let's see, mamma must take the piano-stool so she can gesture. There now, who says I'm not a manager?"

Even Mr. Russell laughed at the girl's vivacity. All were seated as Maud directed, and John Hardy pinched his arm. He really didn't know whether he was in Heaven or at his work.

He soon found out.

"Well, Mr. Hardy," began Mrs. Russell, "it's a

very long story. I don't think you'll need that note-book, for I'll make it simple, and there really is very little in the way of dates and names and places. You know our name, and that's the only name you need to remember, and you certainly know New York, and that's the only place involved; so what's the use of notes?"

John put up his book, and Mrs. Russell went on. Horace shut his eyes, and Maud held his hands like a vice.

"Ten years ago," said the lady, "I went to England, from my native city, New York, a widow with my little Maud, then eight years old and very delicate. Mr. Russell met us, and nine years since, this very month, we were married. Three months ago, on my husband's fifty-third birthday, we gave a grand holiday party to the hands of his factory, and everything was going on splendidly, when I accidentally stumbled on him in his study, with his head on his desk, crying like a baby. It was the third time I had found him so. The other times I went away quietly, thinking it best not to disturb him, but this seemed so strange I really couldn't resist the impulse to speak. I did so. At first he parried my questions, but finally told me about a little boy he had lost in New York twenty years ago; how he never slept without dreaming of his child; that in his thoughts by day and his hours of wakefulness at night the little fellow was ever present; that bitterest self-reproaches were constantly heaped upon him, and that over all his life of prosperity and success hung this dreadful mystery, like a pall of blackest gloom, and at times he felt he should go mad in sheer despair."

"And you," said the detective.

"I," replied Mrs. Russell, "I saw my path as plain as daylight. In less than ten minutes I had the master among his men, the happiest of them all, for I had settled it then and there that his duty and my pleasure were one. His duty was to find that boy; my pleasure was the same—and that's why we're here."

"Yes, Mr. Hardy, that's why we're here," broke in Maud, "and that's why you're here, which is much more to the point. Only I don't see that mamma has told you as much as she might have. For instance, mamma, don't you remember how papa says he was just at the lower end of a park, and was looking at a picture of a fat woman and a zebra on a great banner across a street, when all of a sudden little Harry was gone?"

"Perhaps Mr. Russell can give me the details of the loss, now that I have heard the story of your coming," said Hardy, and taking his note-book from his pocket received from Horace Russell the particulars of the eventful night, when all that made life dear and sweet to a loving mother and a happy father was in an instant blotted from their sight.

Then as he rose to leave the detective said: "First of all I'll hunt up the police blotter and find out all they knew at the time of the disappearance."

"And then," said Maud.

"And then, Miss," replied he, "we'll consider our course."

It was arranged between Mr. Russell and Hardy that the latter should call every morning at nine, and report every evening at eight, and that whatever happened should be disclosed in full at the latter hour.

Bidding the Russells good morning, John Hardy found himself hurrying down town to the Central office, as if wings were on his feet, and ether in his lungs.

The man thought he was interested in his mission.

Perhaps he was.

He certainly was heels over head in love with Maud Russell, and didn't know it.

CHAPTER XI.

SOME STRANGE DEVELOPMENTS.

WHEN Hardy reached Headquarters he reported at once to Superintendent Matsell the developments of the morning, and was gratified at the great interest the old gentleman took in the matter; especially, when upon comparing dates it was found that little Harry had been lost when Matsell was Chief of the Municipal Police, some twenty years before.

Reference to the official documents afforded nothing beyond the bare fact of loss, and so far as any practical help was concerned, the books might have been burned years before.

This much was ascertained—no dead body answering Harry's description had been found at or near the time of his disappearance, and on that they based a hope that he was still living.

"It might be well, Hardy," said the Chief, "to examine the records at the Tombs. Suppose we go down there now"—and jumping on a Bleecker street car, down they went.

Warden Quinn stood at the open gateway of the City Prison, as the Superintendent, in full uniform, gold spectacles and high hat, stepped upon the sidewalk. A second after John Hardy appeared from the car, and together the officials walked up to the Warden, who saluted them with a calmness of demeanor which very inadequately pictured the wonder of his mind.

"Ah, John, good morning, John," said Matsell, addressing the Warden. "Hardy and I have a little business with your old books this morning. How long will it take Finley to get down the record book of 1854? I want to see it. Let's see; we want August. Tell him to get us the August record, John, and then show us through the prison."

The Warden gave the necessary orders to the kindly-faced keeper, who has been on duty at the Tombs, man and boy, since the first prisoner was taken inside its dreary walls.

The three then passed the keeper at the inner gate, who respectfully touched his hat as he facetiously proffered return tickets to the Superintendent and the Detective, and walking along the stone-covered enclosure, reached the entrance to the prison for men, just as that relic of barbarism, the "Black Maria," was driven in for its morning load of island prisoners.

The "Black Maria" is a heavy wagon, shaped like

a windowless omnibus. At the extreme top is a slit, extending around from front to rear, and immediately back of the driver is a small hole. Through these utterly inadequate orifices air is supplied to the people shut and locked in, on their way from the Tombs to the island ferry. Men and women, old and young, drunk and sober, filthy and clean, innocent and guilty, the hardened offender and the neophyte in crime are packed into this noisome van, as sheep were formerly crowded in the cattle cars, before the happier days of Henry Bergh and his Society for the Prevention of Cruelty to *Dumb* Animals.

Who can exaggerate the scenes possible in that hideous vehicle? Instances of horrible brutality and physical outrage are of frequent occurrence, and every trip makes known its report of blasphemy and indecency, wicked and repulsive in the extreme. The Commissioners of Public Charities and Correction are good men and kind. They love their families, and give humane directions to their subordinates; but what do they know of the actual life of the prisoners nominally controlled by them?

Take this very small part of the daily routine, the transfer of criminals from the temporary to the permanent prison. They see it done every day of the year; they see the rude conveyance, the brutal keeper, the unfeeling driver; they know that men and women are crowded into the narrow, unventilated, stomach-turning coffin, like pigs—they know and see it all, as their predecessors did for thirty years before them, but they make no change, effect no improvement.

And if there is this indifference to matters directly before their eyes, what are the probabilities of the ten thousand horrors concealed from their gaze, kept out of sight by cunning officers, or perpetrated when the superintending eye is turned away? The holiday story of our public institutions is often told, and paraded at length in the columns of our papers, but the great everyday suffering—that's as yet unwritten.

The Warden's quick eye saw the disgust pictured on John Hardy's face, as sixteen hideous looking brutes were packed in the wagon, and turning his attention, said to Mr. Matsell: "Well, Chief, it's rather a novelty to see you down here. What's up?"

"That's a fact, Quinn," replied Mr. Matsell, "I really don't believe I've been here before in six months. I know very little of the details of our office. It isn't as it used to be. Bless my heart! Why, in the old time the Chief knew everything, and did pretty much everything too. We didn't have any political Board to bother us. The Mayor was head of the police, as he ought to be; and head of everything, as he ought to be. But he never interfered with me. Many's the time I've put on an old slouch and dove down amo: g the roughs, wormed into their secrets, been arrested and taken in, and never found out till the magistrate ordered me to take off my hat in the morning. In those days, John, a Chief was a *Chief.* Talk about this uniform; why look at that picture hanging in the office when you go back. It's a picture of me in the old fashioned uniform, hat and all. That *was* a uniform, and it meant something too."

"That 'twenty years ago' seems to stick in your crop, old man," said Warden Quinn, as he gave a sly wink at the detective.

"Yes, yes it does," said Matsell. "The Mayor was saying to me only a few days ago, that with all our 'modern improvements' he thought there was really less security on the public streets now than there was then. It seems harder to get the right kind of men on the force. Politicians boss the whole job, and it's simply impossible to move on the works of some of the worst criminals in the city, with success. They know all about our purposes about as soon as we do who make them. You'll be surprised to know what I am here for now. Oh! good morning, Mrs. Foster."

This salutation was in honor of the matron of the prison for women, a good dame of perhaps fifty years of age, combining keen qualities of head with kindly graces of heart; and as rigid a disciplinarian as any martinet in the army of tradition.

Mrs. Foster has been matron of the prison thirty

years. She is one of the few persons in New York official life who hold position on account of fitness Wardens may come and wardens may go, but matron Foster holds on forever. With the unfortunate she is kind, as becomes a woman. With the vicious she is stern, as befits a matron. She tolerates no breakage of her rules, but looks with great favor on the erring sister who would be glad to do better. Mrs. Foster is not so famous as Florence Nightingale, but her sphere is as important and her mission as holy. Were she relentless and cruel, as many women are, she could make the Tombs a hell. Were she a gossip, as many women incurably are, she has it in her power to retail evil enough about New York to afford the press sensations for a decade.

She's no such person.

Advancing with a quick, elastic step, she cordially greeted her old friend the Superintendent, nodded hastily and pleasantly to the Warden and the detective, and invited them into her sitting-room.

After a moment's rest they passed through a narrow passage into the Female Prison, white and clean as constant scrubbings could make it, and chilly as a tomb. On the left of a contracted corridor were a number of small cells, most of which were empty. In one of them was a "Drunk"—a young hearty-looking woman, who, fighting and screaming, had been pushed in but a short time previous, and falling flat upon her face soon passed into a dull and heavy sleep She was brought in by a policeman, too drunk to care for anything or anybody; naturally a good-hearted girl, gin made her a demon.

She was full of it, and from her shapely lips fell such terrible profanity as made even the accustomed ears of the matron and her assistant, Mrs. French, shrink with disgust.

Her bottle was taken from her pocket, and when the Warden and his guests looked through the iron grating her heavy snore resounded through the hall, and beastliness seemed perfectly disclosed.

This is not the forum for a lecture on temperance —but that sight was a text from which lectures might well be drawn.

It is true enough that women and children, as a rule, suffer from the intemperance of their husbands and parents, but no one who is unfamiliar with the police blotters of our station-houses, and the sad records of the lower courts, and the fearful scenes witnessed every day in every year by the prison officials, can understand the extent to which whiskey drinking is carried by the women of this generation.

Surely intemperance is the Sin of the Time.

Every fashionable saloon, has its patrons on whose tables light wines sparkle. At the parties of our "best people" wine is offered in the supper room, and young men find stronger stimulants in their retreat above. The lady who accepts the invitation of her friend to dance, finds herself in an all-embracing aroma of punch or toddy. On the cars, one constantly sees little flasks produced, turned up and emptied. Every hotel's finest apartment is its bar room, made brilliant with gorgeous adornments and magnificent fixtures. From the earliest dawn of New Year's morning to the last flicker of December's stars, wine and rum, and whiskey and gin are regarded by many as Heaven's best gifts to man.

Pious men rent their stores for gin mills.

Christian gentlemen pay their pew rent from incomes derived from the traffic in liquor.

And are women so different that the temptations of palate and physical sensation which fascinate men, are powerless over them?

Let the Tombs answer.

Go to Blackwell's Island and examine the sickening record.

We have Societies for the Prevention of Cruelty to Animals, and Associations for the Conversion of Foreign Heathens, but it seems to us that if ever there was a need for societies and associations now is the time, and this the sphere of operation.

Old and young, male and female, are on the broad road to death and destruction,—and rum is the devil who leads them.

Mrs. Foster's iron steps were bright as a new dollar.

At the head of the staircase is a circular corridor, white-washed and damp, from which open cells like those on the lower tier. In these are always crowded many girls, the majority of whom await trial, or are serving short sentences of ten to thirty days. Now and then one has a book or a paper, but as a rule, they sit or lounge all day and sleep all night; the hardened and the beginners together, with no distinction of any sort or kind between them.

It is all wrong--but how to remedy it is a huge problem.

As the party passed along to a private reception-room at the end of the corridor, Mr. Matsell said: "Mrs. Foster, I came down to-day more especially to see, if by reference to the old records, I could find out anything about a little boy who was lost twenty years ago this August. I was Chief at the time, but all I can recall is that the papers made quite a fuss about it, a small reward was offered, and nothing came of it. I thought there might possibly—but it really isn't probable--be some clue from the books here. Ah! here's Mr. Findley with the record."

The keeper handed the Record-book to the Superintendent, who adjusted his great gold spectacles and slowly turned the pages until he found the date.

There were "drunks" and "disorderlies" by the score, two murders, a few burglaries, the customary allowance of milder offences, but no clue to a lost boy. Ordinarily there would be no sense in looking at the Tombs' books for such a record, but it will be remembered that neither the police memorandum nor the coroner's office furnished any information whatever, and the only other chance was that little Harry had been taken directly before a magistrate and committed by him to the temporary care of the warden.

Under the head of August 21st, appeared this entry:

Name: James Delaney.

Age: 45.

Occupation: Builder.

Residence: Stranger.

Offence: Drunk.

Sentence: 10 days city-prison, $10 fine.

Remarks: When brought in had small boy, five years old, with him. Boy sent in to Foster. Discharged after two days' detention, and fine remitted by Dowling.

"Let me see that," said Mrs. Foster.

Seizing the book the good old lady put on her glasses, ran her finger over the entry, and then gave a long whistle.

"Bless my heart. That's the same boy," said she. "Why, French and I have talked that child over and over a hundred, yes, a thousand times. He was the dearest, sweetest little fellow you ever saw, and he no more belonged to that Delaney than I do. The boy seemed to like him, too, but there was something about them both that didn't hitch. I had the little chap right in this room and I held him right in this chair. I rocked him on my lap, and all I could get out of him was 'I want my mamma,' or 'where's papa?' He wouldn't tell his name, except 'Bub' or 'Bob,' so we called him 'Bob.' I got Dowling to let the man go for the child's sake—you can always manage Joe Dowling through his heart—and when they went off the fellow was sober and ashamed, and the tears stood in his eyes because they fixed him up a pass for Chicago, and a kit. Remember that boy! I remember him as if he sat before me this blessed minute."

"God bless my soul!" said Matsell.

The Warden, though a kind-hearted man, was too much accustomed to sensations, to be particularly affected, but Detective Hardy, who was young and enthusiastic, jumped at what he clearly saw was one end of a clue, which might lead him to professional success, and perhaps aid him in making an impression on the young lady at the Clarendon.

Even while copying the record and making memoranda of the matron's story, John Hardy's active imagination was building castles in the airy future.

He saw—what is there that young men and women do not see at such times?—fame, fortune, success in all that makes life worth the living, all absolutely in one's grasp, almost. How often we wake from sunny dreams, so real, so true, that they challenge physical experience itself in reality, only to find that they *may* be, but are not, true.

But Hardy was hopeful. He had a royal physique. Every movement, from the flash of his eye to the tread of his foot, showed spirit. He thought quickly, spoke well, bore himself as became a man, never forgot his position, and was one of the few men in this queer world, who have sense granted them before they have wasted life, and lost its opportunities in experience.

He knew perfectly well the social difference between himself and Maud Russell, and that she had seen in him simply a means of bringing peace and comfort to her father's heart. He knew that she cared no more for him than for the driver of her carriage. And, to do him justice, he had not as yet detected in himself any feeling deeper than that of admiration for a very beautiful and winsome woman. But for all that, he was conscious of an influence, an attraction which made him think, and was gradually affecting his purposes and plans.

Taking down all that the record disclosed, and making full notes of all that Mrs. Foster could recall concerning Delaney and the little "Bob," Hardy said to the Superintendent that he thought he would go to the Hotel, and see Mr. Russell, although he would not be expected until eight in the evening.

They parted at the entrance, the Superintendent

going down to meet the Mayor, with whom he went every noon to eat clams in Fulton Market, and the detective to the Clarendon.

CHAPTER XII.

THE SNAKE IN THE GRASS.

JOHN HARDY reached the hotel at four o'clock in the afternoon. Mr. and Mrs. Russell were out driving, but Maud, knowing the arrangement between her step-father and the detective, inferred that this call must be a matter of importance, and directed the waiter to show Hardy to the parlor.

When Hardy entered, Maud advanced to meet him with an eagerness born entirely of her interest in his mission. He was disappointed and pleased to hear that Mr. Russell was not in, but deeming discretion the better part, simply said that he would call later, and made his adieu.

As he left the room, a gentleman in the undress uniform of a naval officer entered, and greeted Maud with earnestness and evident delight. Hardy looked long enough to see that the interest was reciprocal, and with a muttered disgust hurried away.

Holding Maud's hand in his, William Templeton

drew the fair girl to a seat in the window, partly concealed by the heavy drapery, and sat beside her.

"Well, dearest," he began, "is it true at last? Have I really found you, and is it possible I hold your dear hand in mine, uninterrupted for a moment? Really, it seems too good to be true."

Maud smiled sweetly, and after a moment's lingering, drew somewhat away from her ardent lover and laughingly said: "There, Will, that must do for now; how fortunate that you should see me here; do you know who that person is I was talking with? He's a detective, and is going to help father find his little boy."

"His little boy?" echoed Templeton.

"Yes, his little boy, lost ever so many years ago," replied Maud. "Papa hasn't seen him in twenty years, and he's determined now to find him, if it's a possible thing."

"Well, don't waste time in talking about little boys," said Templeton. "If he has as hard a time in finding a son, as I have had in trying to find a father, I pity him, that's all."

William Templeton was a waif.

He was found in a Massachusetts work-house by a benevolent party of Boston.

By him he was taken to the Hub, educated and fitted for college. When the civil war fever broke out, William was fond of the water, and begged his friend to get for him a commission in the navy. He did so, and the lad entered the regular navy as ensign, and at the end of the war ranked as Lieutenant, with an unusual record, creditable to him as a man and a sailor.

His protector died shortly after, leaving him a small fortune. The lieutenant went to Europe on leave of absence, and on his trip home met and admired Maud Russell.

Together they promenaded the Cunarder's deck long after the old folks had "turned in."

The moon, the skies, the ships in the distance, the astronomical perplexities, the sea serpent, the phosphorescence in the water, the gulls and the passengers were for them a never-failing source of interest and conversation.

She became entangled. Her affections went out toward this stranger, and he was greatly taken with this charming English girl.

Men are curious creatures, and take the oddest possible fancies.

Everybody on that good ship liked William Templeton except Horace Russell, and Horace Russell was the only man for whose good-will William Templeton cared the toss of a copper.

When Maud or his wife appealed to him to be more courteous towards Templeton, Mr. Russell became insanely angry. He gave no reason for his dislike, all he knew was that he would not like him, and he forbade his wife and daughter even to speak to him, in the improbable event of his crossing their path after reaching the city. Mrs. Russell's influence over her husband was great, because she rarely exerted it. He was a good man, and although very set in his ways, was never deaf to sensible argument.

In this matter Mrs. Russell quietly told her husband that his opposition to Lieutenant Templeton's steamer attentions seemed rather strained. The man held a position of honor, and was well spoken of by every one who knew of him among the passengers, and as he would doubtless soon have his own affairs to attend to, it was not likely they would be in any way embarrassed by him.

Mr. Russell was not convinced, but he was silenced, and as Maud, who was really very fond of her new-made friend, was wise and prudent enough to avoid any scene that might annoy her father, there was no further cause of trouble on the voyage.

Templeton was a brave officer and a bad man.

In the service he was esteemed for the qualities that endure under privation and trial. He had won his way unfavored by politicians, the bane of every public department, and his theory of life had condensed into one hard maxim : Let every man take care of himself.

With all his bravery and pluck, in spite of his good

nature and happy-go-lucky manner, he had a weakness.

He loved money.

No man ever made fortune honestly in the service of his country. Templeton was not morally above certain grades of dishonesty, but he had never been in position to take or speculate, or falsely audit; he had his pay, and a very meagre income from the estate of his adopted father; but the most rigid economy would not make him rich, and he hated economy.

He was about twenty-six years of age, and at a time when most men are trustful and genuine, had become suspicious and deceitful.

He deliberately planned his future, basing it on a marriage with money—give him the money, and the rest he was willing to risk.

He saw Maud, he liked her; he thought her the daughter of the rich manufacturer, and believing her to be his heir, resolved to win her.

Introductions at sea are easily obtained, and when Miss Russell and Lieutenant Templeton bade each other "good-night," after their first introduction, they were as well acquainted as many people would be only after many years of friendship.

Maud was a queer combination of prudence and indiscretion. She had just passed her eighteenth birthday, was bright, sweet-faced, and elegant in manner. She had the air of a beauty and the innocence of a pet; she idolized her mother, and Mr. Russell had found in her the most loving of children.

But she was fond of admiration, and so fond of it that a close observer could see that she catered for it.

Some men and women are born flirts, and flaunt their purposes before the public eye, careless of the world, and reckless of its opinion, so long as their own "good time" is assured.

Maud was not one of those. She shrank from vulgarity of manner, or vulgarity in display, as quickly and as naturally as from rudeness of speech. And yet there was a curious boldness about her which manifested itself in an over desire to please, the motive being, whether she knew it or not, to gain thereby the flattering income so grateful to her.

She was as gracious to the steward as to the captain; she met the detective with the same smile that beamed on Templeton. Compliments pleased her, come from where they might. And if a beautiful face, a distinguished air, and a kind heart with a winning smile, would not elicit compliments in society, what would?

She had had but little attention at home; indeed, there were but half a dozen families in the town, and the Russells, though well-informed and living in good style, were not on visiting terms with the older county families.

Still Maud knew something of life, and her regular

trip to London brought her more and more, year after year, into the cauldron of social excitement. She read some, was fond of music, played the piano tolerably well, rode dashingly, and was esteemed an acquisition at the parties she attended.

Of course she received at such times much attention.

Every woman has more or less of it, and it is by no manner of means determined either in quality or quantity by the prettiness of the face. There are thousands of doll-featured girls who go through life without attention; and in what circle do we not find a plain face the recipient of all the courtesy and civil ity possible. It is evidently what there is behind the face that attracts.

However, Maud was very beautiful and winning as well. Her manner was bright and jolly, her heart sunny, her general air that of contentment. She was greatly pleased with the attentions of her friends, but she had never met a friend who had taken such perfect and all-absorbing possession of her as William Templeton. He seemed to know by intuition what were her desires, and he never hesitated to gratify them.

In spite of the dislike of Mr. Russell, Mr. Templeton found frequent opportunities to be with Maud on the steamer, and when they reached New York, although no formal engagement had been made, both felt that their betrothal was but a question of time and prudence.

As they sat together on the sofa, Maud becoming apprehensive of her father's return, said: "Why can't we go out for a walk or a drive? It is *so* long since I have seen you, and I have so much to say to you."

Templeton was only too glad to go. He rang the bell, ordered a carriage, and Maud went to her room.

The Lieutenant believed Maud to be not only the daughter, but the only child of Mr. Russell, who always spoke of her and to her as "daughter," so that her remark about the "little boy" meant more to Maud's lover than she could have imagined, or he would care to have known.

He was very fond of Maud, but fond or not, he had determined to marry her, and thus gain her father's wealth.

Presently she appeared, perfectly equipped, and leaving the Hotel by the 18th street exit, entered the carriage and drove off towards the Park.

"Maud, tell me about this 'little boy's' business," said Mr. Templeton. "What is it, who is he, any way, and how is it I never heard about him before?"

"Well, I declare, Will, that's *rather* a long string of questions, I should say," replied she; "but as we have plenty of time, and you are so good as to give me this delightful drive, I'll tell you all about it. And then, too, if you only *could* help us, papa would love you just as I do."

She then gave Templeton a narration of the story so familiar to her and the reader, and by the time they had reached the Mt. St. Vincent Hotel in the Park, he had mastered it all, and was quite prepared to say to Maud : "Suppose we stop here for an ice;" and to himself, "this is just precisely my luck. I only wanted this to make assurance doubly sure. Three cheers for me—and the 'little boy!'"

CHAPTER XIII.

A TERRIBLE TEMPTATION.

THE evening of this bright summer day was full of events.

1. Lieut. Templeton had secured a pledge from Maud Russell, that she would consider herself his betrothed, and him, her accepted lover.

As yet, and indeed until Mr. Russell's antipathy could be conquered, the engagement was to be secret from her family.

2. Detective Hardy had made his report to the Russells, and found to his surprise that the stern, quiet-mannered Englishman, was a perfect fire of enthusiasm, kindled into flame, and outburst by the meagre story the detective had to tell of his morning's gleanings.

3. Mr. Russell had outlined a plan of operations, including an immediate trip to the West, the offer of a large reward through the Chicago police, and such other operation as a review of the ground might suggest.

4. And last, but by no means least, Maud in her

good-night letter to her lover, wrote to Templeton every word reported to Mr. Russell by the detective, as well as the entire programme for the future.

Bidding Mr. Russell and the ladies good-night, and promising to take the anxious father to see Mrs. Foster early the next day, John Hardy pulled his soft hat over his eyes, lit a cigar, and moved slowly down 4th avenue. Just as he reached 14th street, he was accosted by a gentleman, who, touching him on the shoulder said: "I beg your pardon, sir; are you Detective Hardy?"

There was no reason for Hardy's denying his name, and yet his professional caution was on the alert, and his suspicions were aroused. Hastily glancing at his companion, he was about to answer, when the light from a street lamp disclosed the handsome features and manly figure of Lieut. Templeton. The detective placed him at once, but pretending not to, replied: "Yes, sir, that's my name. What of it?"

"That depends," rejoined Templeton. "If you have half an hour to spare, come with me, and we will discuss a matter of some interest to both of us—and perhaps of profit. Where shall we go—Delmonico's?"

"No Delmonico's for me!" said Hardy. "That'll do well enough for pleasure. If you want to talk business, where you can be as noisy as a Bedlamite, or as quiet as Greenwood, come with me."

"I'll do it," said Templeton; and he did.

A short ride on a 4th avenue car took them tc Houston street, and a shorter walk led them to the door of Harry Hill's noted resort for all sorts and sizes of pleasure seekers of New York and vicinity.

Passing through Hill's wonderful stable, where he keeps trick ponies, educated dogs, and wonderful sheep, and through the dimly lighted bar-room, they reached a flight of stairs which led to the concert-room.

Templeton had never been there before, and wanted to linger; but to the detective it was an old story, and calling Harry Hill, a stout built, cheery faced Englishman, to him said: "Harry, this gentleman and I have a little matter of business to talk over. Let me have the use of your parlor for a few moments: that's a good fellow."

Harry Hill took a good look at Hardy's companion, shook his head as if half in doubt, and preceded the two to the room.

The average man living in New York knows about Harry Hill's saloon; its Punch and Judy, its dancers, and singers, and boxing matches; its free and easy opportunities for safely seeing a great deal of what young men call "life;" and the fact that it is one of the regular "shows" of the city. But probably not one in five hundred of Harry Hill's visitors could correctly picture even the outer characteristics of the proprietor's inner home.

Pictures of prize-fighters, fancy sketches of noted boxers, bronze horses, flash story-books, foils and gloves, brass knuckles and billies were the paraphernalia which rose before Templeton's mind, when he thought of the probable adornments of the home of Hill. As matter of fact what Templeton saw was as follows: Two very fair specimens of Kaulbach's skill, several fine photographs, and one or two admirable English engravings hung on the walls; in one corner was a small boudoir book-case bearing standard literature from the Bible to Hume, from the book of Common Prayer, to Byron and Thackeray; in another a larger table and desk, fitted with writing materials, and ornamented by curious Japanese ware; in the centre was a handsome round table, with books and cigar case, while two doors opening outward disclosed a dressing-room and a bed-chamber.

Templeton was astonished. Mr. Hill saw the look, and smiling, said: "A trade's a trade, my friend. ''Arry 'Ill 's one thing 'ere and another there. That's all," and shutting the door left the two men to their business.

Neither cared to begin, but Hardy, lighting a fresh cigar, threw himself on a lounge, and Templeton was forced to take the initiative.

"Mr. Hardy," said he, "I am a friend of the Russells, and aware of their plans. They are in search of a little boy Mr. Russell lost some twenty years ago. And I am that boy."

"WHAT!" cried Hardy, and jumping from his seat like a greyhound, banged his hand heavily on the table, and stared through Templeton's eyes down to his very soul.

"Don't make a noise, man," continued the Lieutenant, "you would do yourself greater credit if you listened. I say, I am that lost boy, and you can prove it—if you care to. Old Russell has heaps of money, and can be bled like an ox, for anything that is genuine. He loved his child, lost him carelessly, left him cruelly, and mourns him sincerely. I know he would spend $100,000 to find that son. And I think if you were to find him, your fortune would be insured. Now listen. I can satisfy you that I am Russell's son, and your business will be to convince him. Is it a bargain?"

For a moment Hardy was nonplussed. He had met many rascals in his police experience, and had worked out many a plot, but the cool impudence and suicidal audacity of this putter-up of villainy, eclipsed all previous examples of the kind.

He thought rapidly, and concluded it would be well "to lay in" with Templeton until the plan was ripe. Nothing could be gained by bluffing him; much might be learned by pretending to work with him. After a brief pause, he said:

"I don't know you, sir. Are you quite certain you can satisfy me?"

"Of course I can," replied Templeton with a cunning smile; "of course I can, and I'll agree to put it off for six months too. How will that suit your royal highness?"

"Perfectly," rejoined Hardy; "you have my address. I shall be in town two or three days, and then we're off to Chicago. Come in and see me when you're ready to talk finally;—and now let's see what Harry has to show us to-night."

Together they passed into the saloon, and taking seats at one of the little round tables, made part of a large and laughing audience, listening to the jokes and songs of the character-people on the stage of Harry Hill's.

CHAPTER XIV.

FIRE, FIRE, FIRE.

THAT night Horace Russell seemed a boy again. Long after his customary hour of retiring, he walked his parlor, talked earnestly and rapidly of his plans, read and reread the slips cut from the papers of twenty years back by his former wife, told for the one hundredth time the story of little Harry's loss, and worked himself and Mrs. Russell into a state of excitement bordering on frenzy.

Maud had long since kissed them both good-night, and went to her room to write to her lover.

With her long, soft tresses hanging over the bed, she was a pretty picture, when her mother, entering the room, found her on her knees in prayer.

Folding her in her loving arms, Mrs. Russell said: "Darling, don't think to deceive your mother. You are more deeply interested in Lieutenant Templeton than you care to confess. Tell me, darling, is it not so? and if so, let me know exactly how you feel, and what your relations are with him. Conceal nothing from your best friend. Tell your mother all."

Maud, as we have seen, was bright and quick, even pert and almost forward at times, but she was truth itself in speech, and this one secret of her heart was all she had ever sought to keep from the mother she idolized, and for whom nothing could be good enough.

She had promised Templeton to be his wife, and to keep her promise secret.

What should she do between her mother and her lover.

Right was with the mother, but might seemed to be with the lover.

"Has he told you that he loves you, dear?" said Mrs. Russell.

"I know he does," evaded Maud.

"And how does my darling know so much?" continued Mrs. Russell, as she pushed a little closer to the citadel; "did he tell you to look in his heart and see?"

"No, darling mamma," replied the girl, "he didn't say that, but please, mamma, don't ask me any more questions. I cannot tell you; really, I cannot say another word. I do love him, mamma. He's as brave and noble as he can be, and he loves me so dearly. Don't be angry, mamma darling. Don't be angry. We can wait, you know, ever so long; and besides he's going to help find little Harry. He said he would, and he will; and if he only could find him and make papa happy, what a splendid thing it would be for all of us. And he likes you too, mamma!"

"Mrs. Russell smiled faintly at her daughter's enthusiasm; but, taking her head in her arms, she pressed her warmly to her heart, apprehensive for the future, for she knew the feelings and passions and bitter prejudice of her husband.

"Come, my dear," called Mr. Russell from the parlor, "you mustn't keep daughter awake all night. Let her go to sleep. Good-night again, little girl."

Mrs. Russell rejoined her husband in his planning, and it was quite one o'clock ere the consultation ended, and even then they were undecided whether it was better to go to Chicago, or start the search in New York city itself.

The entire hotel was resting quietly at three o clock in the morning, when the cry of "Fire! Fire!" startled the sleepy watchman on the corner of the avenue, and a policeman, who was resting against the iron rail, actually knocked three times for help before he opened his eyes.

Smoke was rushing in volumes from the upper windows. The story below that was in flames.

Clerks ran hastily through the house to arouse the people, servants were driven from their rooms in the attic, children were bundled out of the house, and efforts were made to save the baggage of the guests. The adjacent streets fairly hummed with excitement.

Crowds thronged about the firemen, the engines puffed and snorted and whistled, while the quick buzz of the wheels made merry music on the air.

If there is any one thing existing which resembles a fully developed, fiery devil, with wings of flame and a blazing tail, it is a modern fire engine as it flies to the scene of disaster, with its bells and whistle, and steam, and smoke, and screams, and dash of speed along the streets.

Half a dozen of these wonderful machines were at work, and the conflagration was largely under control. Still the building was burning, and great clouds of smoke overhung it and permeated every room.

Mr. Russell had been, for many years, in the habit of waking very early in the morning. As regularly as the seasons in their course, Horace Russell rose every morning of his life at three, looked over at his mills, drank half a glass of water, looked at the mills again, and resumed his sleep.

When at sea, his mind worked the same way.

And in pursuance of this habit, he woke on this morning just as the porter in the lower hall discovered the smoke. By the time the other guests were fairly awake, Mr. Russell had his wife and Maud downstairs, and was hurrying them into the street, when Maud, eluding his hand, slipped by him and ran in the direction of their rooms.

Half wild with fear, Russell did not at first know

what to do; finally, and quickly, however, he gave his wife in charge of an officer, and directed her to walk down toward the Everett House, while he flew to find Maud. The halls and staircase were flooded with smoke. Guests rushed down-stairs half-dressed, with such things as they had hastily caught up. The hotel people were shouting and directing. The police were in the way as usual, and the firemen worked like heroes.

If ever men earned their pay, these fire laddies of the paid department earn theirs, and ought to have it promptly.

Blind with the smoke, half paralyzed with apprehen sion for Maud's safety, and really anxious about her mind, Mr. Russell felt his way to their apartments. They were filled with dense, black, stifling smoke. Groping to the window, he stumbled and fell on the body of his adopted daughter. Desperate, and half conscious only, he instinctively grasped her in his powerful arms, and sought the door.

Had he overestimated his strength?

Possibly, but not his love.

Love for the dear girl who had caressed his weariness to sleep at the close of many an anxious day, who had brought sunshine to his heavy heart in many a time of gloom, gave him inspiration, and he achieved in an automatic way, half heedless of what he was about, an act of heroism which, under other circum stances and for another person, would have made him famous. Staggering towards the door he fell. Half rising, he dragged the unconscious girl on and down the single flight of stairs separating their apartments from the ground floor, step by step, till together they attracted the attention of men at the entrance, and the cheery voice of John Hardy said: "Brace up, Mr. Russell, brace up, old man; it's all right, brace up."

And he did brace up, but, overcome with smoke and excitement, fell exhausted on the stones.

Hardy had turned for a moment to give some directions to his partner, as they called the detective who worked with him, but seeing that Mr. Russell could no more "brace up" than Maud could jump up, he extemporized a litter for them both, and had them carried along through the crowd down to the Everett House, where Mrs. Russell had ordered rooms, and was waiting pluckily to meet them.

Mr. Russell soon revived, and after a glass of brandy felt quite like himself, and wanted to see Maud.

But Maud had been put to bed, and in her hand, tight grasped, her mother found the cause of her return to her room—a little gold brooch in which was a picture and a lock of curly hair.

The picture was Templeton's; so was the hair.

CHAPTER XV.

TROUBLE IN THE HOUSEHOLD.

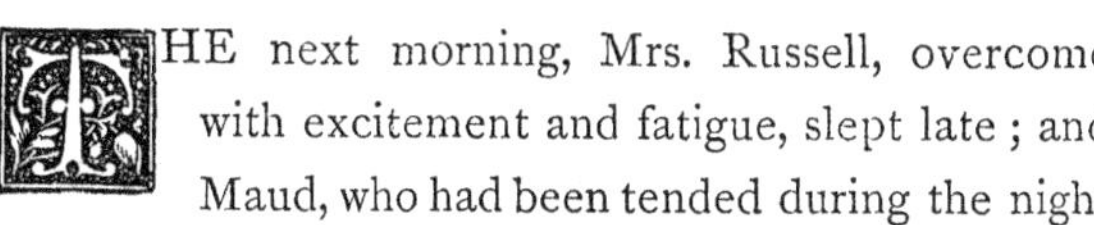

THE next morning, Mrs. Russell, overcome with excitement and fatigue, slept late; and Maud, who had been tended during the night by her mother, rested at her side.

The detective called at ten o'clock, and finding Mr. Russell in the reading room, was surprised and delighted at his freshness and vigor. Together they walked to the Clarendon, arranged for a transfer of the luggage, which was in no way injured, and then, in pursuance of their agreement, drove to see Matron Foster at the Tombs.

The good woman was very cordial in her greeting, and gladly rehearsed the story of little "Bob," adding that it would be the happiest day of her life when she could see him restored to his father's arms.

Mr. Russell was deeply affected both by the story and the interest Mrs. Foster exhibited in the fate of the child; but he did not conceal from himself the great improbability of a successful search for a boy whose life for twenty years had been withdrawn from his knowledge, nor the greater improbability that "Bob" should in reality be the Harry of his heart.

Nevertheless, in the absence of other suggestion, he determined to adhere to his scheme, and go with Hardy to Chicago, even if Maud and her mother were unable to leave the city.

After an interested examination of the prison, Mr. Russell bade Mrs. Foster "good-morning," and, accompanied by the detective, turned towards the door, when, quick as a flash, the sturdy officer dashed into a reception room just inside the iron gate and rail.

As he did so, Lieutenant Templeton handed a pass to the gate keeper, and walked over towards the female prison.

"Did you see that man?" said Hardy.

"No," replied Mr. Russell. "That is, I did, and I did not. I saw some one come in, but was so thunderstruck by your rushing off that I paid no attention to him. Why, who is he?"

"That's just what I want to find out?" rejoined Hardy. "You go on to the hotel; wait there until you see me. Just take the yellow car, tell the conductor to let you out at the Everett House, and you're all right. Excuse me now; every minute's an hour."

Mr. Russell did not precisely see the force of what Hardy said, but though somewhat dubious in his mind as to the propriety of the young man's conduct, did as he was directed, and soon regained the hotel.

Hardy went at once to Warden Quinn's room, borrowed a uniform, put on a belt and cap, and with baton swinging from his wrist, re-entered the prison yard, and walked quietly over to the Matron's office.

Fortunately he met her as she was leaving the wash-house. Accosting her, he said: "Don't start, Mrs. Foster; I'm Hardy, the detective. I have a point to make here. There's a gentleman in your room who wants to see you. If I happen to seem rather curious, take no notice of me. I'm on business."

The sagacious woman twinkled her eyes in token of comprehension, and quickly entered her office.

As she did so, Lieut. Templeton rose from his seat, and advancing with great politeness, extended his hand, bowed, and said: "This is my old friend, Matron Foster, at last. And not a bit changed, either. How kind you were to me, and how often, when a boy, I added to my lisping prayer, 'God bless Mamma Foster.' Do you not remember me?"

"Remember you?" said Mrs. Foster. "No, I don't. How should I? I never saw you before. What do you mean?"

Mrs. Foster is no fool. She has had her eye-teeth cut these many years. She is sympathetic, but not at all credulous. Real suffering elicits her condolence and aid; but bogus complaints could never wring a tear from her, if they were to try a thousand years.

She didn't "take" to this honey-dropping gentleman. He was altogether too grateful, and his gratitude came rather late in life. Had he found her at last? Why, for thirty years she had not left her post! Every day of every year she had opened and shut her room. She is never sick; never away; vacations are an unknown quantity to her, and as for sleep—well, they do say she never sleeps; but that is probably not so.

"No, I don't remember you. Who are you?" said the robust Matron.

"Who am I? Why, I am little 'Bob,'" said Templeton. "Surely you remember little 'Bob' to whom you were so kind in this very room, now twenty years ago."

"Little 'Bob'!" cried Mrs. Foster; "little 'Bob!' little fiddlesticks! *My* little 'Bob' had no such snake eyes as you've got, nor such hair, nor such—oh, don't bother me. If that's what you came here for, you've lost your time. I don't know you, and I don't want to."

"But hear me, madam; I have proofs of what I say," said Templeton, now thoroughly alarmed. "And it may be worth money to you to help me, too. I have reason to believe I have found my dear father, and your aid is indispensable to me."

Just at this juncture, John Hardy, in policeman's dress, appeared at the door.

"Here, officer," said Mrs. Foster, "just tramp this party out of here. He's made a mistake. He belongs in the male prison, I guess, and if he had his deserts he'd go there."

Hardy raised his cap.

Templeton looked up quickly, turned black as his boot, and muttering a curse, hurried rapidly by his tormenter toward the gate.

Hardy stopped him by a whistle, and then taking him into the Warden's office, said: "Mr. Templeton, I give you just four hours in which to leave New York. If I catch you here after that, I'll go for you; and what that means you know. Now, get out."

And he got out, right away.

That evening Mr. and Mrs. Russell were dining in their parlor, and Maud, still very weak, was reclining on a lounge, thinking of Templeton, longing to see or hear from him, and wondering how it could be possible for her to convey to him information of her situation, and the necessity of his being content not to see her until she should be able to get out and about, when a servant handed Mr. Russell a letter.

Not having seen the detective since his singular conduct at the Tombs, Mr. Russell was wondering why he did not hear from him, when the letter was brought in. Without looking at the address, Mr. Russell broke the seal.

He read a sentence, turned the page, read again, and then, with a face white with rage, went to the door, opened it, shut it, looked at the feeble girl upon the lounge, and sank despondingly in his chair.

Maud's eyes were closed; her soul was with Templeton.

But her mother saw her husband's passion, and knew that nothing but his love for Maud kept him quiet.

"What is it, Horace?" said she.

"Read that," said he; "read that, and see what an infernal scoundrel you've cherished between you. Oh, that I had him here! Oh, that I had him here!"

His raised and excited voice roused Maud from her reverie.

She, too, knew her father's ungoverned passions and trembled when she saw them upon him. Her sweet voice rarely failed to calm him, and her gentle caresses were many a time and oft the balm which brought peace and comfort to a disturbed circle and a troubled mind.

"Why, papa darling," said she, half rising from her position; "what has happened? Don't look so black; tell me, papa, what is it?"

"What is it?" replied Mr. Russell. "What is it? You're it. Your mother's it. Heaven only knows

5

who isn't it. I must think this out. It puzzles me, I can't understand it. I leave you together. When I return, I must and shall know all."

Without another word the angry man left the room.

And he left two sad, and crushed, and sorrowful hearts as well.

The mother, heart-sick for her daughter; and the daughter, conscious only that something terrible had happened, but what she knew not.

As the door closed, Mrs. Russell caught her daughter in her arms and, wild with grief and apprehension, said: "Sweetest, you cannot wonder at your father's anger, nor at his anxiety. This letter is from Lieut. Templeton to his betrothed bride. Think of it."

"Give it to me, mother," said Maud; "how dared he open it. Mother, give it to me; I"—but she could go no further.

Her mother bathed her head, and kissed and soothed the young girl's temper down.

Then together they read

THE LETTER.

FIFTH AVENUE HOTEL, NEW YORK, *August* 21, 1873.

"Maud, my darling, my own betrothed, I have but a moment to write you and I have volumes to tell you. I have heard, darling, of your night of peril, and although I cannot see you, I understand that you are quite well, though weak to-day. I have to leave town at once. Danger, of which I cannot safely write, threatens me. I had hoped to be of service to your father, but it cannot be. I leave, and leave at once. Consider, darling, my proposal. You are virtually my wife. Why can you not be so absolutely? If you are strong enough, and can manage to elude the vigilance of your over-anxious mother for an hour do so, and meet me in the corridor near the ladies' entrance. I will be prepared with a carriage, and in half an hour's time my sweet-heart will be my bride,—my darling will be my wife. I beg you will not, at this crisis, hesitate or yield to scruples which can only delay what must happen sooner or later. You love me, do you not? Then prove it. Bear in mind, darling, that I *must* leave town. Shall I go alone? And if so, may I not at least carry the picture of my wife with me? I can think of no mode by which I can be informed of your purpose, so I will, at all events, go to the rendezvous, and trust to the promptings of your loving heart for a favorable response. And till then, sweet one, darling, *adieu.*

"Ever yours,

"W. T."

"Great Heavens! Papa will meet him, and"—

Again Maud fainted, and her thoroughly frightened mother threw water and lavished kisses upon her until, half dead with fear, she opened her eyes, and whispered, "Save him, save him!"

Mrs. Russell was not a woman of the world, nor a society-woman in any sense. She was born in New York City, and at the age of thirty-four was a widow, with a daughter six years old. With the child she went to Europe, traveled two years, met Horace Russell, then a widower, at the house of a London friend, and at the time of the present occurrence, had been Mrs. Horace Russell ten years.

She was a clear-headed, kind-hearted woman, very fond and proud of her husband, and idolatrously devoted to her daughter. Like her daughter, she was the incarnation of truth, and nothing of whatever moment or consequence had ever been, or could ever be, a temptation to one or the other to swerve even by a look from the line of perfect veracity.

But here was her daughter—and there was her husband.

Without a word, she kissed Maud on the forehead, left the room, and passing quickly down the private stairway, stood near the ladies' entrance, her figure partially concealed by the curtain of a window.

Would he never come?

Moments seemed ages, and her courage was oozing fast when the well known form of Lieut. Templeton appeared at the head of the staircase.

A slight movement of the curtain attracted his watchful attention and, in a moment, he was at the side—not of the loving daughter, but—of the indignant mother.

It was a study for an artist.

But there was no artist there; only two embarrassed and mutually anxious individuals, neither one knowing precisely what to do or say.

Presently Mrs. Russell, with fire flashing from her eyes, said: "Mr. Templeton, we thought you were a gentleman. We find we were mistaken. For my daughter's sake, and that there may be no scene between you and my husband, I came here to tell you you that we decline all further acquaintance with you, and to assure you that no member of our family has the slightest desire to see you again. Now go, and go quickly, unless you care to meet Mr. Russell, for there he comes, and with him the detective."

Without a word, Templeton, who was thoroughly alarmed, hurried away, while Mrs. Russell quietly regained her room, and drawing Maud's arm through hers, gently led her heart-broken daughter to the privacy of their chamber—and what passed there, we may imagine, but certainly cannot know.

CHAPTER XVI.

WHAT NEXT? THE PROGRAMME.

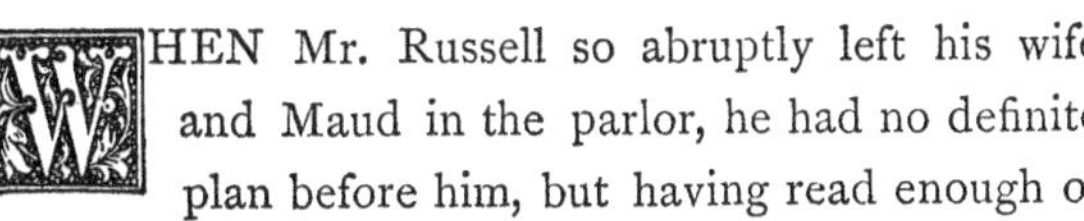

WHEN Mr. Russell so abruptly left his wife and Maud in the parlor, he had no definite plan before him, but having read enough of Templeton's letter to get a general idea of love and an engagement, and only so much, he saw the absolute necessity of his being alone for a few moments, ere he trusted himself to speak.

He understood his own passionate nature thoroughly, and being very anxious about Maud's physical condition, wisely and kindly checked his outburst and simply left the room.

His meeting with Hardy at the door was purely accidental, and without alluding either to Templeton or his letter, Mr. Russell entered at once upon a discussion of their Chicago plan, as together they passed within twenty feet of his wife, on their way to the general parlor.

Hardy was in trouble.

He had seen but little of Mr. Russell, but he liked him, and was interested in his mission. Still he knew so little of the man, that he was in doubt as to the advisability of telling him about Templeton's proposal at Harry Hill's, and the exposé at the Tombs. The detective felt competent to manage Templeton in any scheme he might attempt, and as yet knew nothing of the condition of affairs in the family. He had seen Maud and Templeton together and had noticed the warmth of their greeting, but the only thought suggested by that, was the difference between Templeton's social opportunity and his own—a thought which had often made him curse the world, which, even in epublican America, is disposed to be sensitive on social points.

Hardy's maxim was: "When in doubt, hold your tongue;" and, being in doubt, he obeyed that teaching, believing that if at any time it became necessary to bluff, outwit or confront the plotter, he had the game in his own hands.

Unsuspicious, then, of Templeton's design upon his fortune, Mr. Russell, as calmly as he could, canvassed the possibilities of a search at the West, while Hardy, uninformed of the new development that had upset the peace and harmony of his employer, quietly aided him. During the interview, Hardy presented this programme for Mr. Russell's action, as the best he could, after consultation with the Chief, suggest:

THE PROGRAMME.

1. Obtain official letters of introduction from the mayor and police to the Chicago authorities.

2. Obtain personal letters to people of prominence from the New York correspondents of Mr. Russell's mills.

3. Go to Chicago with Hardy, secure a local detective, offer privately or through the press, a small reward for information, leaving all negotiations in the hands of Hardy and the western officer, and then be guided by circumstances.

"That's not very long," remarked Hardy, "but it's the boilings down of many an hour's thought. The old man has given time and consideration to this matter astonishingly. If ever you want to interest Matsell, just connect your subject with something that occurred twenty or thirty years ago, and he'll jump in lively."

"Well," replied Mr. Russell, "it seems sensible. The only point is that we seem to be giving up New York altogether. This 'Bob' search may be a farce and result in a fizzle. If so, we waste our time and throw away our money—although, to be frank about it, money is really no object. Do you know, Hardy, that boy of mine would be only twenty-five years old now; yet, from the agony and suspense that I have been suffering ever since, a *hundred* and twenty-five years it would appear to be. God knows I have but the one wish upon my heart. I miss him all the time; I think of him, dream of him, talk to him—but always as my baby, my Harry boy of twenty years gone by.

"Come, come, this won't do; I'll see Mrs. Russell and the doctor. As soon as they say Maud may travel, off we go.

"Now, Hardy, I need hardly assure you of my earnestness in this life-work. I trust you. In any event your reward shall be ample; but if we succeed, your heart's desire shall be granted—I'll make you rich and independent for life. Now go, my friend, learn all you can from the prison people, and get all needed letters from Mr. Matsell; I'll attend to the rest. Good night."

Hardy bade Mr. Russell "good night," and Mr. Russell went to get it.

He found the gas brightly burning in the parlor, and the door of Maud's room shut. He entered his own chamber. The bed was undisturbed; evidently his wife was with her daughter. Knocking gently at Maud's door, Mr. Russell waited for an answer.

None came.

He softly opened the door and on tip-toe approached the bed. Fast asleep in her mother's arms lay the beautiful girl, with flushed cheek and eyelids wet with tears.

Mrs. Russell's eyes were wide open, but she dared

not stir lest Maud should be disturbed. She saw love in her husband's smile, and as he bent over her to press a father's kiss upon the "daughter" of his heart, though not of his race, Mrs. Russell whispered: "Good night, father; I will stay with Maud—she is very nervous, but all will be well. Good night."

For a moment Horace laid his hand upon her brow, then kissed her tenderly, and, without a word, left the weary and the comforter together.

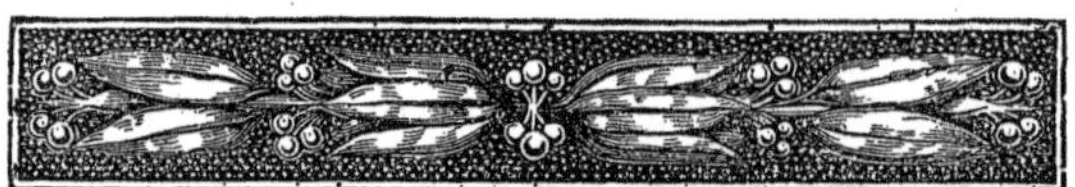

CHAPTER XVII.

THE SCENE SHIFTS. THE TEMPTER AT WORK.

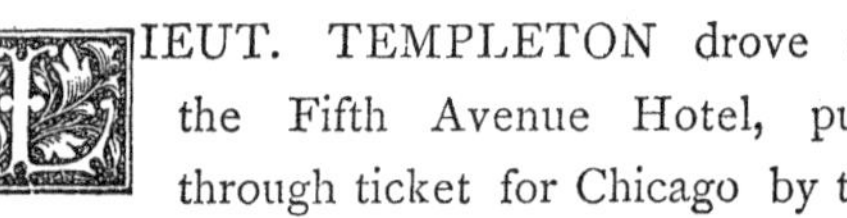

LIEUT. TEMPLETON drove quickly to the Fifth Avenue Hotel, purchased a through ticket for Chicago by the morning express, paid his bill and left orders to be called in time for breakfast and the train.

The evening he occupied in looking through all his papers, and deliberating as to what was best for him to do with his commission. He was liable at any hour to be ordered on duty, and resignation after the receipt of orders would not be tolerated: or rather it would subject him to such criticism in naval circles as he would not care to brave. And then, too, it must be borne in mind that Templeton was not so foolish in his ordinary life as he has shown himself in dealing with Hardy. He doubtless believed that the average policeman, of whom Hardy was a type, had only to be approached, to be secured. A bribe, he thought, would never be refused unless it were too small, and he had purposed making his offer to Hardy so tempt ing as to be irresistible.

He failed.

What Hardy, or the average officer might do under some circumstances we know not, but Templeton's manner was unfortunate ; his time was badly chosen, his plan was too startling—and, besides, the detective had warmed towards Mr. Russell, and the sweet face of Maud was constantly before his eyes.

Having failed with Hardy, Templeton's next hope was to work on Maud's affections through her fear for his personal safety, induce her to marry him, and then leave or take her with him, as might seem best at the time.

He failed in that also.

Had the letter been handed to Maud, it is quite certain she would have met her lover ; and had she gone, weak, nervous and unsettled as she was, it is more than probable she would have yielded to his importunities, and placed herself at his disposal, and brought desolation on her mother's heart.

From that she was spared, but at what a cost!

Failing in his second endeavor, Lieut. Templeton bethought him of a third and better scheme. He knew Mr. Russell perfectly. And he was well informed of the plans, as arranged in general by Hardy and Russell before the morning of the fire. With this in mind he was discussing the advisability of resigning his commission in the service, that he might risk all he had in one desperate venture—a claim to the right and title of Horace Russell's son.

He took time to think of it, and pondered it well before he decided.

He then wrote his resignation and had it mailed at once.

His trunks were packed, his travelling preparations made, his bed ready.

And he slept like a boy till the porter called him to rise.

In due time, Templeton reached Chicago and on the following day placed himself in communication with the detective office at police headquarters. Securing an introduction, through a hotel clerk, to Charles Miller, or, as he was there more familiarly known, "One-eyed Charley," he made an appointment with him at the hotel, at which time, as he told him, he would lay before him a matter directly in the detective's line of business, and in which there was "big money."

One-eyed Charley was a character, and not altogether a good one. He was very much esteemed by his superiors, his intuition being remarkably clear and his experience great. He knew all the regular thieves and professional men well. His twenty years' dealing with the counterfeiters, and burglars, and minor rascals of the Mississippi Valley had educated him to a point of sharpness and cleverness that entitled him to higher rank in the office than he ever held, but he had risen as far as he could, for gin was his failing, and rum was his delight.

Half the number of sprees in which Miller indulged would have "broken" a less useful man. He knew it, and accepted his lot without a murmur. It was rumored, now and then, that there were other potent reasons for the lack of promotion, but they never rose above a whisper; for much as men might suspect, fear of Miller's vengeance kept the tongues of his bitterest enemies quiet.

He had two daughters, the only living beings for whom he cared the value of a rush—for whom he saved what he could; and that was by no means inconsiderable.

Physically, he was ugly. His head was well covered with a reddish thatch; in a fight he had lost his left eye; his face was badly marked with traces of small-pox, and in stature he was tall when he sat, and short when he stood. Morally he was queer; he believed in no God, no heaven, no hell, no future of any kind; his motto was "keep all you get, and get all you can." Mentally, he was shrewd and quick; shrewd enough to see that, in his business, honesty, as a rule, was much the best policy, and quick enough to see when he might safely serve a dishonest purpose with profit to himself.

And this was the man who called on Lieut. William Templeton at his elegant apartments, in pursuance of an agreement made at the general office.

Templeton saluted Miller, as he entered the room, with: "How are you, my friend; what will you take to drink?"

"Well, sir," replied the detective, "I don't mind a stiff rum and gum, after we've finished our talk; but if you mean business, defer the refreshments till business is done. My chief clerk is my brain, and liquor is his worst enemy."

"All right," said Templeton, "as you say; but you surely will let your chief clerk have the flavor of a good cigar under his nose, won't you?"

"Yes. I don't object to that; but I really think as how that curious creature would very much prefer a pipe, if it's handy," rejoined Miller; and, suiting the action to the word, drew from his pocket a common clay pipe, filled it with "horse cut," lit it, and puffed vigorously.

"Now, young man, as the widder said, pitch in, and what you've got to say, out with it."

Templeton eyed him closely.

Under any circumstances he would have done so, but his experience with Hardy had taught him a lesson, and he meant to profit by it.

He eyed him closely, and concluded he would do.

Miller pretended not to notice the scrutiny, but he

saw it all, and made up his mind that there was deviltry in the air, and he meant to profit by *it*.

Pulling from his pocket a huge wallet filled with papers, Templeton settled himself in his chair and opened the ball.

" Mr. Miller," said he, " I have a long story to tell you, and I want you to listen to it carefully, professionally, and *in my interest*. To that end I hereby retain you, and ask, *is it a bargain?* "

With this he laid five $20 bills upon the table, pushed them over to Miller, and waited for his reply.

Miller puffed quickly, counted the bills carefully, stuffed them in his vest pocket, nodded to Templeton, and simply said, " Go ahead."

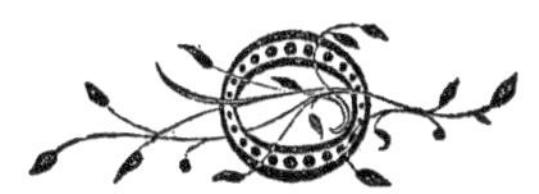

CHAPTER XVIII.

TEMPLETON'S STORY.

UNTIL yesterday," began Templeton, "I was a lieutenant in the navy. My resignation was forwarded last week, and last night's mail brought me official notice of its acceptance. I see you think a man who has so pleasant a berth is foolish to get out of it. Well, possibly, but I have two strong motives, and one equally a motive but not so strong.

"First, I want money.

"Second, I want a father.

"Third, I want a wife.

"The way to each and all of these, I believe, lies through my resignation, whereby I am left free to prosecute a plan, in the outwork of which I need your aid.

"Don't misunderstand my position. I am not poor. In any event I can abundantly compensate you. My game is higher and my prize greater.

"Who I am, no one knows.

"Where I came from, no one can tell.

"I may be the son of a beggar, and I may be heir to one of the largest employers in Great Britain. I have chafed under my assumed name of William Templeton till my mind is sore, and, at times, the very mention of it makes me wild. I hate it. I hate its origin and everything connected with it.

"As near as I can make out, I am twenty-five or thirty years of age. I run back connectedly until my tenth year, as follows: thirteen years I have been in the service; four years I was at college and three years I was preparing for college under the protection, and at the home, of a good-natured Bostonian who found me sick and homeless, and with no other name than 'Bill,' in the workhouse.

"Prior to that, and young as I was, I had been a 'bum.' Nothing that you know by observation of the life of a homeless boy, can equal what I knew by daily experience. I've been through it all. I blacked boots, sold papers, ran errands, slept under stoops, in ash barrels and over steam escapes, eat when I had food, and bore hunger when I had none. Dirty, half-clad, bare-footed, often never washed, on the Island in New York, in the Tombs, known to the watch, and often sick, I led the life of a vagabond as long as I can remember."

"Well, I'm blowed," interrupted Miller. "Say, stranger, do you know, I like you. Pitch in again."

Templeton who was too much in earnest to smile, or to welcome the interest, proceeded.

"I have a vague memory of stowing myself on a schooner, but whether it was accidental or intentional, I don't know, and of being very ill. From then, until I found myself in the hospital of the workhouse near Boston, I recall nothing. I have had of late a pleasant life. My associates were gentlemen. Society is always open to a uniform; and then, too, I prided myself on my record. At college, although among the youngest, I ranked well and my protector was so pleased with my general progress that he left me his property when he died, from which I have a small annual income.

I see the power of money—and I want to wield it.

"I see the advantage of family connection—and I think I see my way to it.

"I have met a woman whom I love: and through her boundless love for me, I see the clue to both family and wealth."

"Well, if you've got it all down so fine as this, where do I come in?" said Miller.

"Are you a Mason?" asked Templeton.

"No, I ain't," replied the detective; "and I don't want to be. I can keep a secret better than any Mason can, if that's what you mean."

"Well, that was not what I meant," rejoined Templeton, who was wondering in his mind whether Horace Russell's high rank in Masonry could in anyway baulk his plans.

For several minutes neither spoke, and then, as if inspired, Miller jumped up, and, resting his two hands on the round table, over which blazed four fan-tailed jets of gas, he looked his companion full in the eye, and said: "Stranger, there's something on your mind, and you don't do justice to the subject. When you go to a doctor, you tell him just what's the matter, don't you? Well, then. And when you go to a lawyer you tell *him* the whole story, don't you? Well, then. Now you've come to me. This cash is my fee. State your case. If I like it, I keep the cash and go on. If I don't like it, I keep the cash and step out. That's all. How old are you, anyhow? Don't be a boy."

Templeton smiled at the idea of his being a boy, for he felt as if he had had about two hundred years of experience in the ruggedest paths of life, but he naturally hesitated to repeat the mistake he had made with Hardy, and preferred to feel his way more cautiously with Miller.

Fearing to lose a hold on him, however, and with a desperation born of the reckless adventure before him, Templeton determined to lay the case in detail before the detective, and trust to luck to get it out plausibly and successfully.

Taking a cigar from its case, he walked to the mantel, struck a match, lit his weed, and, leisurely returning to his seat, apparently resumed his narration, as though there had been no interruption.

"This woman whom I love," said he, "is the daughter of an enormously wealthy Englishman. His name is Russell. He owns and runs immense mills and factories in the interior of England, and is said to be worth five or six millions. He used to live in Michigan, and has, like most men, a romance.

Twenty years ago he lost a son in New York, and he is fool enough to believe that he can find him now. He has no clue to his whereabouts. He knows absolutely nothing of him. He is in New York now, with his wife and daughter, and, before long, is coming to Chicago with a New York detective to look up an old party who was sent out here by the authorities, having with him a boy somewhat answering the description of Mr. Russell's child. Of course he can't find either of 'em—unless we help him!

"I believe I am that boy.

"You believe I am that boy.

"And we must make *him* believe I am that boy.

"What do you say?"

Miller said nothing for a moment.

Then he pulled from his pocket an oblong shaped document, and, opening it carefully, read it to the astonished Templeton, as follows:

HEADQUARTERS POLICE DEPARTMENT,
CHICAGO, *August* 30*th*, 1873.

SIR :—In conformity to the enclosed request from the Superintendent of the New York police, you are hereby directed to place yourself and services at the disposal of Horace Russell, Esq., who, accompanied by Officer Hardy of the New York force, is expected to reach this city some day this week. You will report daily at these headquarters.

Per order of the Chief,

J. G. NIXON, *Clerk.*

To Detective Miller.

The enclosure, a copy of a letter from Supt. Matsell to the Chicago Chief, read as follows :

DEPARTMENT OF POLICE,
NEW YORK, *August* 25*th*, 1873.

SIR :—Mr. Horace Russell, a reputable and responsible gentleman from England, in company with detective Hardy of our force, will call on you in the course of a week or ten days, advising you by telegraph the day before, for aid in a matter of some delicacy and importance. I am desired by the Mayor to say that any assistance afforded Mr. Russell, will be well bestowed. We have done what was possible here and have assigned him the keenest man in the detective bureau. Whatever expense is incurred, Mr. Russell will defray. Commending him to yoûr professional and personal regard, I am

Very respectfully,

GEO. W. MATSELL, *Sup't Police.*

To Chief Police, Chicago.

The fire died away from Templeton's cigar.

But the fire in his eyes fairly glowed with excitement.

"What do you think of that?" said Miller, as he replaced the documents in his pocket. "Ain't that a stunner? How's that for a lone hand?"

Every nerve in Templeton's body was alert. He was in Miller's power for good or ill. With him, fortune was assured; without him, he was worse off than ever. What to say he knew not.

Miller paced the room for some time.

Then he stopped as if he had been shot.

Turning quickly, he said: "For Heaven's sake, man, do you really care anything for that girl?"

"Of course I do," said Templeton; "and, what is more, she is my affianced bride, and it's only an accident that she's not my wife."

"Why, don't you see that you're to be her brother, you fool?" shouted Miller.

"Great God! I never thought of that," said the astonished Templeton, and he sank back in his chair, utterly dumbfounded.

Had he known that Maud was Mrs. Russell's daughter by a former husband, his perturbation would have been less—but that was something he had yet to learn.

Miller quickly brushed that aside, and evincing even more interest in the plan than Templeton had dared to hope, said: "Now, my friend, this sort of thing is new to you, very evidently, for you have told me nothing whatever of your relations to the Russells, nor how you became informed of their purposes."

Templeton then made a clean breast of everything, and gave a clear and connected report of his acquaintance with the family on shipboard, his betrothal with Maud, his gleanings from her of Mr. Russell's loss and search for little Harry, and, last but not least, his wily endeavor to bribe Hardy, before he had really laid out his plan of operations or knew how to utilize him.

"And this Hardy is the same 'Officer Hardy' referred to in these orders," said Miller.

"Certainly," replied Templeton.

Taking a sheet of paper from Templeton's portfolio on the table, Miller rapidly wrote, crossed out, wrote again, read it carefully, aud then said:

"Templeton, I like you. Never mind why; but I do. Some time I'll tell you. I think I see my way here. But there are three embarrassments.

"And you are the chief.

"Detective Hardy is the next.

"And that sweetheart is the third.

"You must all be got rid of, or the plan won't work at all. Now, my idea is this:

"FIRST, I'll take you out of this elegant crib, and give you less ample quarters in the Hotel de Miller. You'll have to keep as snug as a bug in a rug. If Hardy finds you in Chicago, up goes our job. I'd send you away, but there's no telling when you may be needed. It's worth a little trouble, anyhow. So if you agree to it, to my house you go, and in it you stay till I say "come out."

"SECOND, If Hardy can't be bought—and that's ticklish, if what you say is true—he must be managed. Of course, I'll have a big pull on him, as I'm assigned to the job, and if I don't corner him, he must be tolerably wide awake, and New York is too small a place for him; he must stay in Chicago.

"THIRD, I hate to interfere with women. So I won't say anything about the girl till she gets here, and I've got the cut of her jib.

"Now, what do you say? I'll get in for $1,000 cash down, and will take your word for $10,000 more, payable six months after you're the accepted son of Horace Russell. Is it a go?"

"It is," said Templeton; "and *now* what will you take?"

6

CHAPTER XIX.

ONE-EYED CHARLEY AT HOME.

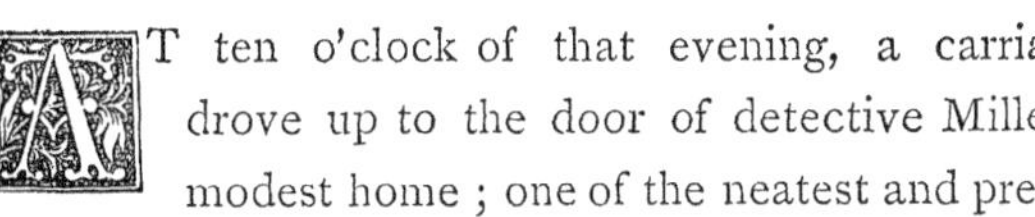

AT ten o'clock of that evening, a carriage drove up to the door of detective Miller's modest home; one of the neatest and prettiest cottages, near the lake. One might easily imagine it to be the "ideal home" of a happy family, whose head and father devoted himself and all his better energies to humanizing his race, and elevating his kind. It stood in the centre of a well-kept enclosure, about fifty feet from the road, and attracted the attention of every passer—it was so clean, and cosy, and inviting.

From the open door-way, a flood of light shone upon the walk to the gates, and thence upon the street.

Miller hastily jumped from the carriage, and, while Templeton followed, assisted the driver in taking the luggage off the box, and into the house.

"Why, father, how late you are," said a sweet voice at the head of the stairs; "and we thought you were lost," said another, while a pair of round arms embraced the detective's burly figure, and a pair of pouting lips gave him a cordial welcome home.

Mary and Martha Miller were twins, and had been partners in this vale of tears and smiles eighteen years. Their mother, a wise and careful Scotch woman, died when the children were ten years of age, leaving them to the curious care of "One-eyed Charley"—abroad, a rough; an indulgent father at home.

Chicago's schools are Chicago's pride, and of the many pupils graduated in the past ten years, none have better records, none stood higher than the pretty daughters of this ugly featured man; and no father in all the great assemblage was more nearly choked with joy and pride than "One-eyed Charley," when his girls received their blue-ribboned diplomas, and joined the class chorus in honor of their Alma Mater.

He was a strange compound, this Charley Miller.

On the very threshold of a great crime, with an accomplice at his side, his mind full of a nefarious scheme, and his thoughts burdened by his plan, he smilingly greeted his daughters, affectionately kissed them, was really delighted to be at home, and looked forward to a few hours' rest and domestic relief, with satisfaction and delight.

His life had been hard and bad.

His companions were often the vilest of the vile.

He prided himself on knowing all the rascals in the West; and if report was to be credited, he was not unfairly classed with them.

But his wife loved him when living, and blest him as she died.

And his girls—they fairly idolized him, and manifested their regard, in every way known to loving woman and ingenuous children.

Miller entered the parlor, followed by Lieut. Templeton.

Mary and Martha stood near their father.

"Girls," said he, "this is an old friend of mine. His name is Harry Russell. He will stay with us for some time, and none must know of his being here. Ann, the cook, can be relied on, as she has been for twenty years; and, when I tell you that it's for my sake and in my interest, that this gentleman shall be made to feel at home, and that his being here is not to be talked about, that ends it. Mr. Russell, these are my daughters. This is Mary, and this is Martha, the best girls in the world; not so pretty, perhaps, as their old dad, but quite as good."

Templeton bowed pleasantly, and, as he did so, wondered how it was possible to tell which was Mary and which was Martha. There was not a discoverable difference in the color of their hair, the calm beauty of their eyes, the shape of their features, or the style of their figures.

"We will see that your room is in order, Mr. Russell," said Mary, as she left the parlor.

"Would Mr. Russell have anything to eat, father?" said Martha.

"Nothing for me, I assure you," replied Templeton; "we dined late, and I am so very tired that I shall welcome most of all a hospitable bed."

Presently Mary returned, saying that Mr. Russell's room was in readiness, and bidding the young ladies "good-night," Templeton and Miller carried their trunks up-stairs.

The room assigned the new guest was not large, but very comfortable and well furnished. From the front windows, he had a perfect view of the broad calm lake, on which a magnificent harvest moon was gloriously shining, and from the side he could look upon one of America's greatest marvels, a vast and populous city, striving with zeal for supremacy in all that is enterprising and beneficent, and cursed with extremest temptations to vice, and the widest opportunity for every species of debauchery and sin.

Templeton had an eye for the beautiful, and gazed long at the silvered lake, ere he unpacked his "room trunk" and prepared for rest.

CHAPTER XX.

SHE WAITED PATIENTLY.

HE sun was high in the heavens when Maude and her mother greeted Mr. Russell the day after the scene at the table, and it was evident to all that an embarrassment lay upon their intercourse. For the first time since her mother's marriage, Maud did not look Mr. Russell in the eye when she greeted him. She was not ill-tempered, but she felt hurt, and could not understand the extremity of her father's antipathy to Templeton.

After a rather uncongenial hour at breakfast, Mr. Russell walked to the window where Maud was standing, and putting his arm about her, drew hei towards him, and said: "Daughter, I cannot bear to have the least shade of trouble between us. Let us be perfectly frank and truthful with each other, as we ever have been, and see if, in any way, we can come together on this subject, which seems to be very near your heart, and which has given me more anxiety than all my business cares for years. Your mother tells me you love this man."

"Oh, father, darling, I do, I do!" interrupted Maud, and bursting into tears, she threw her arms about her father's neck and sobbed upon his breast.

This was more than Mr. Russell had bargained for, but, remembering Hardy's advice at the time of the fire, he "braced up" and bore it like a man.

After a little the paroxysm passed, and Mr. Russell continued:

"I am quite willing to concede," said he, as, like all fathers, he prepared to yield a point he could no longer hold, "that Lieut. Templeton is a fine-looking, well-behaved person. I find his record in the navy is exceptionably good, and although I can learn nothing of his family antecedents, he is a man of some property, and generally liked by his associates. But I don't fancy him. Why, I cannot tell; but I never see that man without a shudder. I'll say nothing about his letter to you. You are old enough to know your own heart; and what reason he had for believing that such a proposition as he made would be acceptable, you know better than I. I have talked the matter over with your mother, who is your guardian, and the only one in authority over you—for, although I love you as if you were my own flesh and blood, I remember always that I can only advise you—and we have concluded that you may, if you choose, invite Mr. Templeton to call here this evening. We will receive him pleasantly, and if he then makes any formal proposition for your hand, I will answer him precisely as if you were my own child, asking such questions as a father with propriety may ask, and putting him on such probation as is both decorous and just. And then, if all is well, my darling shall have her heart's desire, and all my prejudice shall be whistled to the wind. How does my plan please you?"

Maud's generous nature appreciated the sacrifice her father was making on the altar of her love, and thanked and kissed him again and again.

The three were as happy as mortals could be.

At Mr. Russell's suggestion, Maud wrote a note to Templeton at once, and sent it by a messenger to the Fifth Avenue Hotel.

Stupidly, the boy simply left it at the counter, and the clerk on duty not knowing that Templeton had gone, placed it in his box.

Of course, Templeton did not receive it. And equally, of course, as hour after hour passed on, and her lover failed to answer her summons, which she hoped would be to him both a surprise and delight, Maud's feeble physique drooped, and when the lateness of the hour showed the folly of further expectation that evening, she threw her head upon her mother's lap and cried most bitterly.

Neither Mr. Russell nor his wife could furnish apology, excuse, or reason for Templeton's absence. They shared Maud's disappointment to a certain extent, and the constant strain upon her nerves made them anxious for her health, which, of late, had become less firm than when at home.

During the evening Hardy called, but, as between them, nothing had ever passed in reference to Templeton, the perfect explanation he could so easily have given was not made, and a cloud rested on the entire group because of the absence of a man, whose presence to-day, four hours before, would have created a perfect storm of indignation.

As Hardy started to leave, he said: "How soon do you think you will be able to go West, Mr. Russell?"

"That depends on Miss Maud entirely," replied Horace. "We can't afford to have a sick daughter on our hands; can we, darling?"

Maud looked up mournfully enough, and said: "Go when you wish, father. I'm ready to-night, if you say so."

"Nonsense, nonsense!" broke in Mr. Russell. "What you'll do to-night, is sleep. A good night's sleep will bring you out as bright as a button, and to-morrow we'll take a drive in the Park. By Monday next I think we'll be all right, Hardy. Some friends of mine arrived by the steamer to-day. We dine together to-morrow. Next day I'll get my letter of introduction, and you be prepared with your share by Sunday at the latest. We'll take the earliest train on Monday morning. Good-night, my boy, good-night!"

Hardy bade them all "good-night," and walked away full of wonder.

On his way up town he stopped at the Fifth Avenue Hotel, inquired of the clerk if Lieut. Templeton was still there, and learned that he had gone West that morning.

"Gone West!" thought Hardy. "What under heavens does that mean? It isn't possible that he would be so foolish as to try to cut in again. But no; that's too absurd!" and, dismissing the matter from his mind, he lounged easily up the avenue.

CHAPTER XXI.

JOHN HARDY'S STORY—A SUDDEN STOP.

LEASANTLY seated in a Pullman car, the Russells and detective Hardy sped swiftly on their way to the wonder of the West, the pride of Illinois. It was a beautiful morning, and the perfect ventilation of the car kept the party comfortable, in spite of the excessive heat of the day.

Mrs. Russell was a good traveler.

She was burdened with no surplus luggage. A strap held her wraps and those of her daughter; a small valise contained the needed changes of apparel on the road, and by her side were books and papers for entertainment or relief.

"What time are we due at Chicago, Hardy," said Mr. Russell.

"The schedule time," replied Hardy, "is 5.30; but I understand we have lost time, and may not be in till an hour later. I can't say that I care much, for the scenery is beautiful, and now that we are accustomed to the motion of the cars, it's almost as pleasant here as anywhere. I've been thinking for the last hour or so about that boy of yours. What a life he may have led! Perhaps he has had everything 'dead' against him, and possibly he has been helped from the very start. I know how it is myself, and I tell you it makes a great difference to a fellow whether he paddles his own canoe or is towed along by a tug."

"If it's a fair question, Mr. Hardy, which was your lot," asked Mrs. Russell.

The detective colored up a little, and glanced across the seat at Maud, who was half listening to the conversation, and half gazing at the clouds which kindly shielded them from the fierce rays of the boiling sun.

As Hardy looked at her, she smiled, and said: "Oh, yes, Mr. Hardy; do tell us all about your life. It must be a perfect marvel of romance and adventure. I should dearly like to hear it."

"In many respects," said Hardy, "I have had an easy life; in some a very hard one. My business is peculiar, and leads one into queer scenes and among odd people now and then. But, as a rule, I see the same kinds of human nature in men and women you do, and find life in any one sphere is not so very different in motive from life in any other. I have a little property, but I had a very humble origin. I hardly like to tell you that my father was a scavenger, but he was; and he was as good and true a man as ever I knew; kind and indulgent, though very reticent and not at all informed about matters which interest ordinary men. I was the only child, and, of course, had my own way. I really can't remember much about my childhood, and what I do recall is so strangely mixed up with fancies and fables that it is not at all satisfactory. I think the first event I remember, now, is having a blue suit with bright buttons, one exhibition day at school, and speaking a piece before quite an audience. Queer, isn't it? One would imagine that he'd remember some toy, or playfellow, or a thrashing, or some out-of-the-way thing; but I can see father and mother sitting in the Hall, as distinctly as if they were here this blessed minute.

"Mother was a quaint old body.

"Her Johnnie was the apple of her eye, and the core of her heart.

"And how she did sing!

"I can see and hear her sing now. She was a great Methodist, and she had all the camp-meeting tunes and songs at the end of her tongue all the time.

"I never knew father to speak a cross word to her or to me, and I never saw a frown on mother's face till the day of her death.

"I don't give much evidence of it, I know, but I was always ambitious and successful at school, and especially when I saw that it tickled father so. Every time I received a medal he went wild. Every time my teacher gave me a book, or my report was particularly good, he acted as if a new heaven was opened to him. I don't look a particle like either of 'em. I have a very fair picture of mother in my room, but we never could persuade father to sit for one. He seemed superstitious about it. When he died, I was a messenger in the chief's private office. I was only seventeen, and had been there going on two years, when one of the neighbors' children came running over to headquarters—we lived right round the corner—and said: 'Johnny Hardy, run home as quick as you can, your father's got a fit." I rushed into the police surgeon's room, got Dr. Appleton, and hurried home.

"I was just in time.

"The good old man had fallen in a fit at the corner of Prince and Mulberry streets, and was taken home by people who knew him. As I entered the room he opened his eyes and smiled. I was very fond of him and he of me. Said he: 'Johnnie, boy, look out for your mother. Be a good boy; be a good boy, Johnnie,' and falling back, died almost immediately.

"The doctor said it was apoplexy—and perhaps it was.

"He left mother comfortably provided for, and then I had my pay every week, so we got along nicely, but not for long.

"You see they had lived together forty-two years,

and had grown in and about each other's nature so that when one was torn away—and so suddenly, too—the other had to follow.

"She wanted to follow.

"I saw it pained mother to think of leaving me, but all through her illness she thought and spoke of hardly anything else but her meeting and rejoining father.

"Well, she died too.

"In a little while I was transferred to one of the bureaus as clerk; and, as soon as I was old enough, I was made an officer.

"I didn't like it.

"There's too much 'red tape' and 'boss' business about it. And a man has no chance for promotion unless he has friends, and friends are of no use unless they are politicians. I saw enough of it. Politicians keep men from being 'broken' every day in the year. They put them on the force, and keep them there, too. However, I was lucky enough to do some detective work, in which my mother-wit helped me very much more than my experience did, and I was detailed to detective work altogether. I can't say I like it, but I find it pleasanter than being in the club brigade. But I've seen some queer sights in my time."

"Did you ever have anything to do with a real murderer?" said Maud.

"Oh, yes, indeed," laughingly replied Hardy; "murderers are not always such dreadful people to deal with. Not very many years ago, I was one of five men put on a murder scent, and it occupied us three months constantly. The victim was a very old lady, rich and much respected. She was killed in her own bedroom, one summer night; and the room exhibited signs of a violent struggle. After a sensational funeral we were sent for and given our instructions. Each man had his theory. Burglars, or interested parties, must have done the deed. Nothing had been stolen, so I dropped the burglar idea. I believed the woman was killed accidentally by some one who, for some occult purpose, was in her room; and then, surprised, for fear of detection, did a deed he was very loath to do."

"Well, well, go on," said Maud.

"I wish I could," continued Hardy, "but I was never permitted to. Or, perhaps, I shouldn't say that; but it is a fact that every line of search seemed to lead directly to one of the dead woman's nearest friends. I followed clue after clue, and invariably came to the same point. Then I was bluffed, or foiled, or ordered off on some other job, or pooh-poohed, until I found I was treading on toes which wouldn't stand it, and I must get off."

"But has the murderer never been discovered?" asked Mr. Russell.

"No, sir. There is a kind of open secret about it. And it comes up in the papers every little while," said Hardy; "but money, and politics, and social influence manage to keep it down. I believe I could point the man out as easily as I could point you out. But, if I should do it, in the first place, I would forfeit the confidence of my superiors; in the next, I would doubtless lose my position, and last, but by no means least, very likely I should fail to prove my suspicions. Circumstantial evidence which satisfies me might not have weight with the public or a jury."

"That's so," said Mr. Russell; "but do the other friends of the dead woman regard this one of whom you speak with suspicion?"

"Certainly they do," said Hardy, "and that's the very point. They have from the first; and although, for social pride's sake they keep up an external toleration of the man, I suspect in private they despise him, and really have nothing whatever to do with him. Possibly they have struck a kind of domestic balance; and, remembering all the other hearts that would suffer, have deliberately chosen silence and condonation rather than the shame and disgrace resulting from a public trial. Or, again, there may be nothing in it.

"One of the queerest cases I ever met," continued Hardy, "was that of a lady living in Troy. She was rich, or rather her husband was, and owned some superb diamonds. They were lost—she said they were stolen. Suspicion fell on her maid, and the poor girl was arrested. I became quite interested in the case, because I *felt* that the accused party was innocent. I knew the thief would take the diamonds at once to a pawnbroker in New York, so I simply caused it to be known among the professional thieves that, for certain reasons, the detective bureau wished those diamonds found. In less than a week I received information that they were in a pawnshop up town; and, on inquiry, it turned out that the lady who owned them was the party who pawned them. She was short of money and adopted that mode of raising it, knowing that her husband would be very angry if she were to sell them. I was perfectly delighted when I found it out, and compelled her to compensate her servant for the infamy she had put upon her."

"That was just right," said Maud.

"What did her husband say?" asked Mrs. Russell.

"Oh, I don't know," replied Hardy; "I said nothing to him. If she told him, all right; and if not, what was it to me?"

"Were your parents American, Mr. Hardy?" asked Mrs. Russell.

"My father was," replied he, "but I have an impression that mother was English. She had relatives in England, at all events. I have a trunk of her things at my lodgings, which I mean to rummage some time. It is full of books, and newspapers, and letters, which, I dare say, would throw some light upon her early life. At all events, I think I'll devote my first leisure evening to an inspection, and"——

Hardy never finished that sentence.

Ere the words could come the air was dark and filled with smoke. Dust and cinders, and fire and noise, and hissing steam drove life and breath away. Crashing timbers and splitting wood flew in every direction. Over and over and over again the car rolled, and groaned, and broke into confusion.

The people were like dust in the balance. High and loud, and shrill over the shrieks of the murdered men and women, sounded the fierce rushing of the escaping steam, and, for a moment—long as eternal night—hell seemed to have its home on earth and every fiend was busy.

The engine had struck a pile of rails heaped high upon the track, and had bounded from its iron path full tilt upon the adjoining ties. Two cars rolled over an embankment and four were drawn with terrific jolts across the rugged edges of the parallel track.

The uninjured passengers hurried to the relief of their less fortunate companions. The engineer was dead, the fireman joined him later.

Several passengers were very seriously injured.

Mr. and Mrs. Russell were bady strained, Maud was well shaken but not hurt; but Hardy, when extricated from the wreck, though carefully carried to a bank near by, gave no sign of life, and was pro nounced dead by the conductor and the rest.

Fortunately the accident, or rather outrage, was within a few miles of one of the "line towns," and messengers were at once dispatched for aid.

Mrs. Russell and Maud, with other ladies, were seated in one of the ordinary cars, while Mr. Russell, who had become very much attached to Hardy, stayed by his body.

It was well that he did so, for, after a long time, he noticed a tremor of the lips and a partial opening of the eyes.

"Thank God," said Russell, as he applied a flask of brandy to the lips of his friend, and calling for aid, did what was possible to bring him back to consciousness.

A series of fainting fits showed the weakness of the poor fellow, and suggested also the probability of some internal injury.

A wrecking train came up in about three hours with surgeons and help of all description.

The dead were coffined, the wounded cared for, and, when the *débris* was cleared away, the train proceeded slowly on to the station, drawn by the engine of the relief.

Of the wounded, Hardy was the only one whose case the surgeons pronounced dangerous. They decided that he must not be carried further on. He was therefore left at a house where boarders were taken, and a nurse, hired by the company, was placed with him.

Mr. Russell was completely disheartened by what the doctors said, but was somewhat comforted by his wife, who reminded him that they were only two hours' car ride from Chicago, and that, after they had secured their apartments there, it would be easy to run out and see Hardy, and, if he were providentially spared, to remove him, when convalescent, to the city.

The company's officials assured Mr. Russell that Hardy should have the best of care, and having himself made the nurse promise to advise him immediately if his presence was necessary, or anything whatever was needed, he took his wife and Maude, and sorrowfully finished the journey.

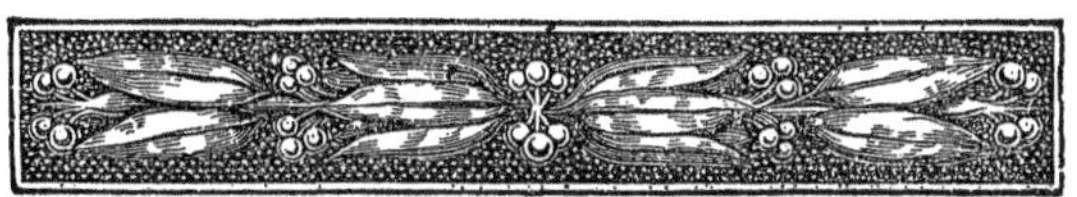

CHAPTER XXII.

THE MILLER AND HIS MAN.

HEN detective Miller brushed his hair down, and paid close attention to his beard, he was not absolutely ugly. Indeed, if he had retained the use of both eyes, he would be tolerably presentable. Ordinarily, however, his short reddish hair would not stay down, and a day's neglect of the razor imparted a tinge to the rude man's cheek which by no means enhanced his beauty.

Two days after Templeton, or, as he was there called, Mr. Harry Russell, was made one of the Miller household, the young ladies were pleasantly surprised when their grim father appeared at the breakfast-table dressed in his best, clean shaven, irreproachable as to linen, and with his hair as slick and smooth as brush and comb could make it.

Evidently something out of the common routine was on the carpet, and Miller's manner made it more apparent.

Breakfast was served, and nothing of moment was

said or done until Miller, who was reading the morning paper and drinking coffee at the same time, choked, coughed, jumped up and spluttered, and then recovering himself, said: "Here, Mary, read this out loud, and the rest of you listen."

Somewhat surprised, Mary took the paper, and read as follows:

"A fiendish outrage, resulting in the killing of several railroad men, the probable death of others, and the wounding of twenty or thirty passengers, was perpetrated on the Michigan Central Railway, yesterday afternoon, about ten miles beyond Johnson station. The New York express, due here at 5.30 P.M., was somewhat behind time, and the engineer was doing his best to recover what he safely could, when he made the sharp turn just below Wilson's Grove. At that point the road is visible but some thirty feet at a glance, and, failing to observe any obstruction, the engineer drove at full speed upon what is represented as a pile of railing. The concussion was tremendous, resulting in the demolishment of the engine, and the instant killing of the engineer. The train was thrown from the track; two of the cars rolled over the embankment, and the rest were jolted at a fearful rate across the rails of the adjoining track. The fireman was drawn from the wreck still living, but he died soon after in great agony. The wounded were attended to as well as was possible by the uninjured passengers, until the arrival of the wrecking train, when all but one were brought speedily to this city, where they were taken at once to the hospital or their homes.

"The passenger who was so badly hurt as to be unable to endure the fatigue of the trip is Mr. Hardy, a member of the New York police force. He was accompanying an English family, who were on their way to this city on matters requiring his professional aid. It seems that Mr. Hardy and the gentleman of the party were sitting *vis-a-vis* to two ladies, wife and daughter of the Englishman, whose name was not obtained. The collision was abrupt and sudden, of course, but Hardy, with praiseworthy presence of mind, caught the younger lady, who sat facing him, in his arms, in such a way as to protect her from contact with the iron work of the seat, by which, as the car turned over and over, he was terribly bruised, while his companions, beyond the shock, experienced no injury of any kind. The surgeons find that Mr. Hardy's left arm is fractured in two places, three of his ribs are broken, his face is badly cut, and his whole body so battered that it is a wonder he lives. He seems to have a strong constitution, and if his mind can rest while his body recuperates, he may possibly recover."

Miller and Templeton looked at each other.

The girls were interested in the romance of Maud's escape.

The men were excited to extravagance of hope by the reality of Hardy's danger.

"What an infernal outrage that is," said Miller.

"Yes," chimed in Templeton; "the fellows who would do such a deed as that would murder their own mothers. Now, what earthly motive could they have for throwing a train full of strangers off the track, and perilling the lives of hundreds of people?"

"Perhaps their object was not earthly," said Martha.

Mary smiled, but the men did not seem to notice her sister's suggestion.

Presently Miller rose, kissed his daughters, and turning to Templeton, said: "If this report is true, it won't be necessary for you to keep so quiet; but wait till I find out. I shall be back, perhaps, at one, but certainly in time for supper. Good-bye."

Leaving home, Charley Miller went first to headquarters and reported. There he learned that the facts were substantially as set forth in the paper, and that inquiry had already been received from New York about Hardy and his condition. The Chief thought Miller ought to go to the hotel at once, and see if he could be of any service to Mr. Russell; so he went.

Mr. Russell received the detective, and in the presence of his wife and Maud rehearsed the story of their accident, words failing only when he sought to picture the noble conduct of Hardy, who had undoubtedly been much more seriously injured in his efforts to shield Maud than if he had cared only for himself. The ladies were also enthusiastic over Hardy, and begged Miller to advise them if Hardy would really be as well cared for where he was left, as if he were brought to the city.

Miller replied that if Hardy was kept quiet for a week or two where he then was, he might be able to endure the jolting of the cars each day a short distance, and then be made more comfortable during his convalescence. He did not conceal from himself, however, the very probable fact that Hardy would not only never see Chicago, but never leave his bed, for the reports received at headquarters said he had passed a very bad night, was in a raging fever, and could not be kept quiet.

Mr. Russell was not prepossessed by One-eyed Charley; but Miller was so quiet, so plausible, so kind in his reference to Hardy, and so blunt in the expression of his opinion, that before the business on which he called was broached, Miller felt that he had the confidence of the family.

And besides he was the detective detailed from headquarters, and presumably as reputable a man as was on the force.

"I suppose," said he, "you don't feel like talking business to me to-day, do you. I called partly to see if I could do anything for you or Hardy, and partly because I am directed to report to you for orders. If it isn't agreeable to-day, I'll call to-morrow; and if you don't feel up to it then, I'll call next day, and so on."

Mr. Russell hardly knew what to say. Whatever thought occupied his mind, was sure to be driven out by his anxiety about Hardy. He wanted to begin his search for his boy, but even that desire brought him at once to the consideration of what he could do without Hardy. Insensibly a feeling of personal regard had grown up between them. Hardy was always respectful, willing, good-natured and sensible. He had tact and knew when to leave.

Few men have that faculty.

He was bright, and jolly, and full of fun, but he was also serious, business-like, and full of resource.

Russell liked him because he was a thorough man of the world, with a clean tongue, and an honest heart.

And the ladies liked him because he was useful, without intrusion, and attentive without gallantry.

Still, much as Mr. Russell thought of John Hardy, it was clear that he could be of no benefit to him now, beyond securing to him the best of care, and most experienced nursing.

That, as we have seen, was attended to, and Mr. Russell concluded that he might as well unfold his plans to the Chicago detective in person.

Mrs. Russell and Maud retired, and Mr. Russell proceeded to business.

"I had hoped," said he, "to have the benefit of Hardy's already acquired information, so that you and he might get to work at once, leaving me rather in the position of one to whom reports are made; but this accident deprives us both of valuable aid, and I find I must take a hand in myself. In brief, my case is this. Twenty years ago I lost a boy in New York. He was five years old. Next day I went home to England. My wife stayed over two steamers, but nothing was heard of the little fellow. She followed me. We nearly died with grief at the time, and the poor girl did succumb at last. Well, twenty years are gone. Harry, if living, is twenty-five years old. I want to find him. Money is no object, time only do I grudge—not that I am unwilling to spend time, and strength, and all to find the boy, but I long to *have* him."

"Have you no clue at all? Couldn't the police help you in any way then or now?" asked Miller.

"Not much," replied Russell; "not much. We did find at the Tombs a record of a man named Delaney, who just at that time was picked up drunk, and taken to the Tombs. He had a boy with him, and was sent out here. Hardy seemed to think it might be well to hunt Delaney up, and trace the boy. It could do no harm, at all events, and might be productive of good. But, as Mrs. Russell says, 'if Delaney was a hard drinker, and had gotten so low as the Tombs, twenty years ago, we are not likely to find him alive at this late day.' What do you think ?"

"Oh, I don't know about that," said Miller; "some hard drinkers live longer than temperance folks. That's nothing to the point. But this boy, what was his name ?"

"Harry," said Mr. Russell.

"Well, Harry," continued Miller, "this boy Harry, did he have anything peculiar about him ? I don't mean curly hair—they all have that—nor anything fancy, but marks or scars, or anything that would *hold.* Look at my cheek. See that scar ? That's nothing but a mosquito bite. I had that bite fifty years ago when I was a baby. I scratched the bite, and made the scar. I don't suppose the little chap had a mosquito bite, but did he have anything at all ?"

"Upon my word, I never thought to speak of it, nor has the question ever been asked," replied Mr. Russell; "but when Harry was in my place in Milwaukee"——

"In where ? In Milwaukee ? Did you ever live in Milwaukee ?" cried Miller.

"Of course I did," said Mr. Russell. "I had a shop there, and turned out the best cold chisels you ever saw in your life. I lived in the city over eight years, and in the vicinity two years more. Why ?"

"Why, my dear sir," exclaimed the detective, who really saw a point in honest search, and certainly saw a bigger point in his little game in Templeton's interest, "don't you see that everything bearing on the boy's early life is of interest? And if you lived in Milwaukee five years with this boy, and he was a boy of any parts at all, he must remember something of his father's home and surroundings. If we were to find a young man who answered the description, and forced us to think he really was your son, unless he could give you some evidence drawn from the experience of his life in Milwaukee, I should very much doubt him. And on the other hand, even in the absence of other conclusive proof, if the youth did remember, to *your* satisfaction, any marked occurrence of the life at home before you lost him, I should yield a much readier assent. I beg your pardon for the interruption, but take my word for it, that Milwaukee life will prove a pivot in this entire search."

What a fortunate thing it is that men and women are unable to read each other's thoughts. There are clever people, now and then, who can make out a little of the inner life of their friends and companions, but as a rule the unknown ground is impregnable.

It was especially fortunate for Detective Miller at this moment; for his lively imagination had already packed itself with facts, drawn from future talks with Mr. Russell, and in turn, Templeton's ready wit was stored with much that would puzzle, embarrass, and delight the heavy-hearted father, and perhaps convince him, that he was the lost boy of his search.

Determining then and there to draw from Mr. Russell all he could concerning his Milwaukee home, Miller settled back in his chair again, and Mr. Russell proceeded as follows:

"Well, as I was saying, I had a little factory, hardly that, and yet it was more than a shop, where I turned out a high grade of tools, and was getting along quite nicely, when I was called home to see my father die. About a year before that, Harry, then four years old, and quite tall of his age, was playing about the place one day when I was out. The hands were busy, and didn't notice him as he went up stairs, where the finished tools were packed for shipment. Presently they heard a sharp cry of pain, and rushing up to see what was the matter, found that Harry had pulled a sharp chisel from one of the benches, and had dropped it on his foot. One of the men quickly took off his shoe and stocking, and ascertained that the little toe of the right foot was cut through, and hung by a mere shred. The stupid fellow cut the little film of flesh by which the toe hung, and hurried with Harry to my house, which was only a block away. My wife bound the foot up, but neither of them thought of the toe itself, till the doctor came an hour later, and then it could not be found. We feared the mutilation would lame him, but he soon recovered, and, really, I don't believe I have thought of it, or of the occurrence in twenty years."

"And yet that very mutilation, as you call it, may preserve you from being deceived by schemers, and fooled by rascals," rejoined Miller.

And to himself, he added: "Off goes Templeton's toe, as sure as fate!"

Mr. Russell then narrated their experience in New York, and concluded by asking Miller if he was willing to begin to hunt up Delaney at once, and to take charge of the whole investigation independently of Hardy, whose recovery was a matter of months at least.

Miller said he was not only willing, but would be very glad to do so. Before making any suggestions, however, he would go home and think it over.

Meanwhile, he proposed that with Mr. Russell he should take the two o'clock train, run out to see Hardy, and return by the train due at Chicago at 9.30. To this Mr. Russell assented, and Miller went to the office to report.

CHAPTER XXIII.

ROBERT DELANEY, CLERGYMAN, APPEARS.

IN canvassing possibilities, Miller found himself confronted by the fact that the old man Delaney *might* be found, and that the boy he was reported to have with him *might* be the lost son of Mr. Russell. To be sure, if, through the efforts of the Chicago police, these people were found, and the object of Mr. Russell thereby attained, Miller would be certain of a large reward ; but he believed a greater profit could be derived from Templeton if *his* plan were to succeed. Already $1000 had been paid to Miller, and $10,000 additional were pledged, but to the shrewd detective's mind, Templeton, as Harry Russell, would prove a perpetual mine to one who held his secret, and could at any time expose his fraud.

Miller determined at once to put all his machinery in motion to discover Delaney; and, first of all, went to the Mercantile Library, where were kept the

Directories of the city for more than twenty years back.

There were quite a number of Delaneys, but no "James" among them until the year 1865, and he was a clergyman. The fact that no James Delaney appeared in the list was not conclusive proof that there was no person of that name in the city; but it was presumptive evidence. In the Directory of 1870 there was "James Delaney, builder;" but after that year, although there were several of that name, none of them were builders.

Miller was about giving up the search, when his eye lit on "Robert Delaney, clergyman." He wondered for a moment why that name should be familiar to him, and then suddenly recalled that at a little Baptist church not far from his own home, his daughters frequently worshipped; and that once or twice the minister, whose name was Delaney, had called at his house.

He further remembered that the only serious discussion that Mary and Martha had ever held before him was about this very man, who had asked Martha to take a class in his parish Sunday-school, and to visit among the poor as a kind of reader to the sick and infirm. Mary thought it was presumptuous in Mr. Delaney to propose such a thing to a stranger; but Martha insisted that the pastor of a church was charged with the Lord's work, and had a perfect right to assume that every person who attended service in his church would be ready and willing to do what he could to aid the suffering and cheer the sick.

The end of it all was, that Martha did not teach in the school, but very frequently called upon the poor people of the district, and in a quiet, womanly way, won the hearts of many sick persons by her gentle endeavors to relieve their troubles, and break the monotony of weary days and sleepless nights.

Miller had heard his daughters talking about these visits occasionally, but it had never occurred to him to say anything about them. He gave Mary all the money she asked for, trusting to her to keep the house books of expense, and knowing that between her and her sister there was no jealousy, and no rivalry, except in their endeavor to make home attractive and pleasing to their father.

The Rev. Robert Delaney was about twenty-six or seven years of age, tall and stout. He walked a trifle lame, but he bore himself with the air of a soldier. Indeed, he had served two or three years in the army, entering as a private, and leaving as a brevet-colonel. He began his service long after the fuss-and-feather days of the earlier years had passed, when for awhile it was easier to be made a brigadier-general than to earn an honest five dollars per diem; but when fighting had become a business, politicians had less and less power every month, and at the close of the war, brevet-colonels really ranked higher in the estimation of men who knew anything, than their superiors whose stars were conferred to please the whim of a politician.

When Robert Delaney began his work in Chicago, he had a small hall and a slim audience; but he was full of zeal, and talked to his hearers as if he were in earnest for their good. He was simple in his tastes, and modest in his manner, but magnetic and impulsive in speech. In prayer and exhortation he was peculiarly impassioned, and his efforts in behalf of young men were so sensible and practical that his reputation soon extended, and, had he chosen, he might have been called up higher many a time. But he preferred to stay where he was and work. His friends appreciated his love of the place, and determined to build him a larger church. This they did, and on the Sunday following the search made in the Directories by Miller, the building was to be dedicated, and the church formally installed in its new home.

Wondering whether he had actually had the very man he wanted under his own roof, Miller made a memorandum of Delaney's residence, and returned to the hotel for Mr. Russell with whom he intended to go to see how Hardy was progressing.

Miller found Mr. Russell in a state of great excitement over a dispatch just received from Hardy's nurse. The message reported Hardy in feverish condition, and said that the doctor would allow no one to see him or enter his room.

Of course, there was no need or use in their going to the place where the wounded man was, if they could neither see him nor do him any good. So the trip was given up, greatly to Maud's regret; who had secretly determined to make one of the party.

"Well, Miller," said Mr. Russell, after it was decided to defer the visit to Hardy, "have you thought of any plan?"

"Yes, sir," replied the detective; "I shall first try to find James Delaney. You told me I think, that the matron said the little boy was five or six years old. How old exactly was Harry?"

"Let me see," said Mr. Russell. "Harry was more than five. I *think* he was nearly six, or he may have been over six and nearly seven. I have no way of fixing his age precisely, except by reference to some of my wife's letters, and I haven't seen them in five years. Anyhow, he was a little fellow, and I should say five, or six, or seven years old—there really is very little difference, you know."

"No," rejoined Miller, "I don't suppose there is. I was only thinking that if living, he must be getting on toward thirty years old; and that, for a driving western man, is the prime of life. Out here, if a man is ever to amount to anything he knows it by the time he turns thirty. I may not see you for a few days. I have an idea. I may go to Milwaukee, and I may go elsewhere. Meanwhile, keep your eyes and ears open, and your mouth shut. If you are allowed to see Hardy I hope you'll go. There isn't much fun in being sick away from home, and ten to one he frets about the job besides."

Maud thanked Charley Miller with her tearful eyes for the kind word he spoke about Hardy. She longed to speak to him about Lieut. Templeton, and to ask if any such name had been mentioned in the arrivals, but she knew better, and did nothing of the kind.

Mr. Russell acquiesced in Miller's proposition, assuming that he knew what was best to do; and after urging him to spare neither expense nor care, bade him "good day," and the party separated.

The Russells drove out with a gentleman to whom Horace had letters, and Miller went directly home.

CHAPTER XXIV.

MILLER GOES TO CHURCH.—A TOE FOR A TOE.

IN pursuance of a suggestion made by their father, Mary and Martha Miller invited the Rev. Mr. Delaney to dine with them the day of the dedication of the new church, and for his convenience six o'clock was the hour named.

At the morning service the sacred edifice was densely thronged, and several distinguished clergymen of the city participated in the ceremonies, the dedication sermon being delivered by the pastor.

Detective Miller astonished his daughtes by volunteering to accompany them to church, and, as in their recollection he had never done such a thing before, it may well be imagined their astonishment was thoroughly leavened with delight.

None of the pews had been rented as yet, and on this occasion all seats were free. The Millers were well known in the society, and, as they were early at the door, were taken to excellent places quite near the pulpit.

The services were rather prosy until the delivery of the sermon.

Up to that time Mr. Delaney had taken no part in the proceedings, and as he sat quite out of sight, Miller began to think he was wasting time.

Presently, however, the pastor approached the desk, and Miller was his most careful observer.

The detective element was in full play.

Miller studied Delaney's head, hair, eyes, mouth, and carriage, as a turfman does a horse.

He examined his points, mental and physical, and confessed himself puzzled.

Is he the son of Horace Russell, or is he not?

There was nothing in Robert Delaney's look or bearing that forbade the supposition, and there was much that might be considered confirmatory evidence, if the theory were already advanced and partially proved.

The young preacher was not a time-server.

He felt himself the bearer of a message from the Ruler of the world, and as he delivered it earnestly and eloquently, self never obtruded, and Delaney never interfered with the envoy.

Little by little Miller became interested in the subject.

He forgot the man in the matter.

And when the minister wound up one particularly impassioned appeal to fathers as exemplars before their children, the old rascal actually found a tear on his cheek, and an uncomfortable sensation in his throat.

Robert Delaney was a sensationalist, but not a vulgar one.

All earnest men and women are sensationalists.

It is necessary that they should be. In this world of hypocrisy and sham, honest endeavor and earnest work win their way and attract attention by their novelty; and whatever is novel is sensational.

The young man succeeded because success was not his aim.

He was popular because he cared nothing for popularity.

He was a good thinker, a magnetic preacher, and thoroughly imbued with the sacredness of his calling, and the universal need of moral and spiritual education. With no other care upon his mind, he had deliberately chosen his field, and now this abundant harvest was rewarding his industry and zeal.

He was loved by honest men, and toadied to by fools; he was appreciated by earnest women, and flattered by silly ones.

The honest and the earnest he loved and appreciated as they deserved; the fools and silly women he understood, and tolerated only because he hoped in time to do them good.

Like all popular men he had his besetting temptations.

Had he been weak-headed, and vain, and selfish, flattery, and incense, and social preferment were at his command.

But he chose the wiser course, and in giving up all worldly plans, in the interest of his Master's cause, he gained the more desirable rewards of respect, esteem and honor of his fellow-citizens and his flock.

He was apparently twenty-six or twenty-seven years of age, with no parents, and no home save the modest lodgings he called his "rooms." Attached to the new church, however, was a small parsonage, and into that he proposed to move at an early day.

His deacons had often told him he ought to marry, but his heart very properly suggested that he should wait until he had met a woman whom he loved.

Delaney had a high regard for his deacons, but there are *some* matters about which even deacons know very little.

He was in no sense a ladies' man.

He thought of women mainly as co-workers in the field he tilled so faithfully.

As teachers, readers, visitors, distributers of helpful literature, and nurses, women were to him a right hand and a left, but no more.

Indeed, until accident led him to the house of Martha Miller he had never met any woman whom he cared to meet or know outside of professional occupation.

He liked Martha.

There was no nonsense about her.

She was genuinely good, and although she had declined to take a class in his Sunday-school, Mr. Delaney was more than gratified at her common sense way of calling on and helping sick people, and especially her happy faculty of brightening up a home of gloom and disappointment. He met her frequently on her charitable rounds, and had on one or two occasions partaken of her hospitality at her father's house, where he had become well acquainted with her sister Mary, and had wondered where under Heaven such a queer-looking fellow as One-eyed Charley had procured two such charming children.

Between Martha Miller and her young pastor no word of love had ever passed.

And not only that, no word of sentiment or anything akin to suggestive remark had ever passed their lips.

Nevertheless—and it is queer how naturally that "nevertheless" follows—close observers were quite convinced that there was an understanding between them, and in spite of the seeming contradiction, it is more than likely that there was a sort of unwritten law, like a social code.

The invitation to dinner had been gladly accepted

by Mr. Delaney, and when his quick eye saw not only the Miller ladies, but their queer old father in one of the front pews, he could not refrain from taking a moment of his official hour for a personal wonder as to what the strange circumstance could portend.

Miller was delighted with the sermon and more than pleased with the preacher.

And as he bent his head when the final prayer was said, he almost resolved to give up Templeton, and, if convinced that the Delaney of Chicago was the little Harry of Milwaukee, to aid Mr. Russell in finding a real rather than a bogus son.

At the close of the services there was the usual hand-shaking of the members and the "buzzing" of the pastor, somewhat increased on this occasion by the peculiar circumstances attending the dedication, and then, accompanied by Miller and his daughters, Mr. Delaney left the church.

It so chanced that Mary walked at her father's side, while Mr. Delaney escorted Martha, a circumstance that afforded Miller food for thought, and added some little weight to the idea which had forced itself upon him during the closing prayer.

Nothing of special note occurred at the dinner table, except that the girls wondered why their father had directed Templeton's dinner to be served in his room, until Miller said: "Mr. Delaney, you are a native of Chicago, are you not?"

The clergyman hesitated a moment and then replied, "I really don't know, Mr. Miller, whether I was born here or not. I have some reason for believing myself a native, and some for thinking I was born in New York. My early life is largely shut out from my memory by reason of a severe illness I had when quite a boy, the somewhat singular consequence of an accident which, though trifling in itself, gave my nervous system a shock, and laid me up for months. From that, however, I entirely recovered, and with the exception of rather an ungainly walk, I suppose I am as hearty and rugged a man as we have. My father, I am quite sure, was English; the name is English, and he had many habits which none but an Englishman could have. He was a builder, and did a great deal of good work here. Poor man! he was very kind to me; and, having no mother, I was his entire family, absorbing all his care and love. His death was sudden and terrible. Possibly you recall it. He fell from a scaffolding on the Episcopal church near the post-office, lingered unconscious but a few hours, and died without a word or sign of recognition. From that time I had a hard row to hoe, but——"

"But you hoed it," interrupted Miller.

"Yes," continued Mr. Delaney; "yes, I *did* hoe it, and save the aid which I got from the All-Helper I was literally my own guide, philosopher and friend. The war gave me an inspiration for good. The physical suffering I witnessed in the hospitals and on the field led me by a natural process to regard the moral degradation and distortion of the race, and I determined if my life was spared to devote myself to the regeneration of my fellows. I am free to say I enjoy my work and take genuine pleasure in its prosecution. I saw so much destitution and depravity result from what I believe to be the greatest curse of our day and generation, that I resolved to make Temperance a distinct and prominent feature of my public teachings. Of course I encountered great opposition, but that's nothing.

"One glimpse of a rescued man's face is ample compensation, and one letter of gratitude from a reformed drunkard's wife or daughter is cheer enough to pay for the abuse of a thousand rumsellers. But you asked if I was a native of Chicago, and not for an autobiography. As I said, I don't know. Father lived in Cincinnati awhile and also in Kalamazoo, and I think in Milwaukee, but he seemed more at home here than anywhere. How long have you lived here, Mr. Miller?"

"Oh, I'm an old settler," said Miller; "both my girls were born here. I'm a western man myself and haven't been east of Illinois in forty years. And I haven't been inside of a church in twenty years that I know of; not that I mean to brag of that before you, sir, but its merely a fact, that's all. The girls attend to that branch of the business, and do it pretty well, too, I judge."

"Yes, indeed they do," said the clergyman, and turning to Martha who sat at the head of the table he entered into a discussion about the church music, in which she was specially interested.

But Miller didn't care about the music. He had his thoughts concentrated on Mr. Delaney's foot.

"Has he or has he not lost a little toe," thought he. And he thought it till it seemed as if he should go wild.

After dinner the ladies led the way to the drawing-room, their father walking slowly in the rear with his one eye bent on Mr. Delaney's feet.

The man certainly limped a little.

But whether the lameness was in foot or leg, Miller could not determine.

He wanted to ask his guest, but he did not dare.

He thought of a hundred different ways of getting at it, but hesitated to put any one of them to the proof.

Finally, in despair, he excused himself, went to his room, took a razor from its case, put two handkerchiefs in his pocket and then knocked at Templeton's door.

Entering he found the ex-lieutenant at full length on his bed reading an official gazette.

Templeton bounded to his feet, and said: "For

Heaven's sake, Miller, let me get out of this for an hour or two to-night. I really *cannot* stand such confinement. If Hardy is mashed, why need I be cooped in my room? I need exercise and *must* go out to-night for a walk, even if it be but for an hour. Come, now, what do you say?"

Miller eyed him curiously and half laughed to himself as he said: "Templeton, how many toes have you?"

Templeton looked at Miller in unfeigned amazement, but seeing no reason to doubt his sanity, and never having encountered in his host even the glimmer of a joke, answered as soberly as he could: "Ten, I believe. At all events I had ten this morning."

"I'm very sorry," said Miller; "that's one too many."

"Well well," rejoined Templeton, "out with it, what's the joke?"

"There isn't much joke about it," said Miller; "I mean just what I said, and further, if you expect to prove that you are old Russell's boy, you've got to prove that you have only nine toes."

"And one must come off?" asked Templeton.

"And one must come off," answered Miller.

"Good Heavens, I can never do that," said Templeton, as he pictured himself in pain, on crutches, lame and, perhaps, disfigured for life.

"But I can," struck in Miller; "it won't hurt. I

can take off your little toe in a jiffy, and can dress it and tend it, and have you all right in two weeks, just as good as new. Seriously, I can. And equally as seriously, if you don't lose your toe, you lose your fortune and we can't afford that; can we?"

Templeton said nothing.

He was a handsome fellow with a swinging easy walk, a firm step and an elastic bearing, born of perfect health and his life upon the sea. He was not vain, but—well, he knew how he looked, as every one does, and was not dissatisfied with himself either.

He knew that the loss of a toe would certainly lame him some, and possibly cripple him more than he could endure. He knew, too, the danger of lockjaw, and he shrank from the mutilation also.

"Well," said Miller, "it takes you a long time to think of an answer. What do you say? shall it be fortune and no toe, or all toe and no fortune?"

"Couldn't we get a surgeon?" replied Templeton, "I am afraid to risk your home-made skill."

"Of course we *can* get a surgeon," said Miller; "and if, when the world knows that Horace Russell, the millionaire Englishman, has found his long-lost son and heir, by means of a lost toe, this blessed surgeon wants to spoil the job, or halve the proceeds, what's to prevent? Oh! by all means let's call in a surgeon. Well, now I guess not. I tell you I can take that toe off just as easy as rolling off a log. It will smart some; but a little healing salve, and careful dressing will cure it up right off, and in ten days or a fortnight you'll be up and about, as lively as a cricket."

"But you haven't told me *why*," said Templeton, who hated the idea of losing even a little toe.

"Oh, I thought I had," said Miller; "the 'why' is very simple. Russell's boy's toe was chopped off with a chisel. Of course he never got another. If he lost his toe then, he hasn't it now. And if you're to be the son, your toe is doomed."

"All right," said Templeton, "get me some whiskey to steady myself with and cut away. All I ask is that you are careful, and do unto others as you'd be done by."

"Why, what's a toe more or less anyhow," muttered Miller.

"Well, it doesn't amount to very much on another man's foot," answered the Lieutenant, "but on one's own its a very desirable feature. Now, you go and get the whiskey."

Miller obtained the whiskey and the salve, and in less than five minutes the toe was off, the salve was on, and the wound was done up in rags and a compress.

Templeton bore the mutilation bravely. Indeed, he acted better than Miller, who was keyed up only by the necessities of the case, and was forced to steady his own nerves by thoughts of the game he was playing and of the stake he hoped to win.

Templeton laid down to rest, and Miller, promising to send one of his daughters to read to his guest, and also to return as soon as Mr. Delaney should leave, went down stairs.

But he had not reached the last step when, in perfect bewilderment, he exclaimed: "How in thunder do I know which was the foot?"

And then he re-entered the parlor where the young women were entertaining Mr. Delaney, or he was entertaining them, and it made but little difference to him, which was the case. If he had known that Harry Russell had lost the little toe of the right foot, while Mr. Templeton had been despoiled of the toe of the left foot, Miller would probably have cursed his luck.

But he did not know it, and, on the whole, he was rather pleased with his success.

While Miller and Templeton were going through their amateur surgery up stairs, Mr. Delaney and the daughter of the operator were enjoying themselves below.

The preacher had a fine voice and sang well.

And Martha had a sweet voice and sang very charmingly.

Mary played and the others sang duets.

Mr. Delaney was fond of Russell's ballads and quite enjoyed singing "The Ivy Green," "The Earl King," and other songs of that style, and the girls were delighted to hear them.

As Miller entered the room, Mr. Delaney was singing:

> "Oh, a rare old plant is the ivy green."

And to save his life the detective could not help saying:

> "Oh, a rare old plant is Templeton's toe."

But he said it to himself, and laughed at his own conceit.

CHAPTER XXV.

MAUD RUSSELL AS FLORENCE NIGHTINGALE.

NE bright morning Maud Russell said to her mother, as they were returning from a little shopping excursion: "Do you know, mamma, I feel quite ashamed that neither you nor I have seen Mr. Hardy since he was brought to town. It will be five weeks to-morrow since he was hurt, and two weeks the day after since the doctor said papa might have him brought to the hospital?"

"Well, dear, what do you want to do?" replied Mrs. Russell.

"I don't know that *I* want to do anything that we all ought not to do," rejoined Maud; "but you must remember the poor fellow wouldn't have been so badly injured if he hadn't tried to save me, and I think we should do all we can to make his misfortune bearable. If you wait for me, I'll buy some flowers and some fruit, and we can call at the hospital to leave our names with the flowers, if we cannot see him."

"Why, my dear girl," said her mother, "your father and I have seen John Hardy every day since he was brought up here. I have said nothing to you about my going, for the hospital, though clean, is a hospital, and you might have encountered some unpleasant scene. Hardy is doing quite nicely. I doubt if he is ever perfectly well, and it will be several weeks before he can hope to walk. I have no objections to taking you with me this afternoon, but we must be sure to be back in time to meet papa on his return from Milwaukee."

"Oh, thank you, mamma," said Maud; "you always let me have my own way without coaxing, and are such a dear good friend. I'll keep right on and get the things, and you order a carriage at the office."

Mrs. Russell went slowly to her rooms, wondering as she walked, whether Templeton's singular absence and more strange silence, were having their normal effect on her daughter's mind and heart.

For a few days after the scene at the Everett House, Maud was greatly depressed.

She was never hysterical, but rather moody.

If Mrs. Russell alluded to Templeton, Maud roused herself and joined the conversation, wondering where he had gone and what had become of him. But both Mr. and Mrs. Russell noticed with pleasure that Maud's pride was wounded and her self-respect hurt so seriously that her mourning for Templeton bade fair, in time, to be relegated to the background.

After their arrival at Chicago his name had not been mentioned but twice, and on each occasion Maud simply asked her father if he had seen any record of Templeton's arrival at any of the hotels.

Between semi-weekly trips to the scene of the disaster, and daily conferences with Detective Miller, Mr. Russell's time had been pretty well occupied, although he had not been unmindful of the social attentions extended him and his family by people to whom he bore letters of introduction.

Mrs. Russell was very quiet in her tastes and domestic in her habits. So much so, in fact, that, were it not for Maud, it is doubtful if she would ever leave her hotel during her husband's absence.

She knew, however, the necessity of keeping her daughter's mind busy, and never refused to go with her either to entertainment or for exercise.

Maud had made a good impression on the friends who had been civil to the Russells in Chicago, but no impression other than that of passing pleasure had touched her in head or heart.

Not that she mourned Templeton as a woman of deeper nature might, but she was worried mentally, and uncomfortable generally about her recreant lover. If she could have known that he was false, pride would have rescued her from grief, but she knew nothing. From the pinnacle of affectionate devotion her ardent admirer had plunged into hiding.

Of course, then, she was annoyed and embarrassed as any other woman would be under similar circumstances.

Mrs. Russell watched Maud's health anxiously, and was delighted to observe her cheerfulness and contentment.

Nothing now seemed to interfere with sleep or appetite. Her color was good and her spirits generally fine. She was amiability itself, and the brightness of her little circle.

While the two ladies were busied in their social rounds, their shopping and driving, Mr. Russell, with characteristic conscientiousness, devoted himself to business.

He had two branches to attend to—John Hardy and the search for his boy.

As already told, Hardy had so far recovered that he was taken by stages to Chicago, where Mr. Russell daily and Mrs. Russell often called to see him.

The other branch was attended to with even greater assiduity and regularity. Mr. Russell had taken a liking to One-eyed Miller, in spite of the first impressions, and after a series of adventures in Chicago, had gone with him to Milwaukee.

There Mr. Russell was bewildered.

His old friends and neighbors had died or gone off.

The town had become a glorious city.

Nothing was as he left it.

Even the place where once stood his modest shop and factory, had been merged into a public park or square, so that it was with difficulty he found it.

Together they remained in Milwaukee several days, during which Miller pretended to gain information about Delaney and the little boy he had with him, and one morning, with flushed face and flashing eye he entered Mr. Russell's room, crying: "Good news, Mr. Russell, good news, sir; I'm on the track at last—thank God, I've struck a trail."

"Is it here?" said Mr. Russell, almost wild with excitement.

"No, but it was," answered Miller, "and it led to New York. Sit down and I'll tell you all about it—unless you want to get back to the women folks to-night. If you do, let's be off."

"Why, of course I do," rejoined Mr. Russell, and together they started for the depot, stopping on the way to telegraph Mrs. Russell of their coming.

"Miller," said Mr. Russell, suddenly stopping in the street, "wait till we get to the hotel. Don't tell me a word till we are all together."

"All right," returned the detective.

At the time Mrs. Russell told Maud she expected her husband's return, there were several hours before the arrival of the Milwaukee train, and entering the carriage, mother and daughter were driven to the hos pital.

Mrs. Russell was so well known to the attendants that no passes were required, and they went at once to Hardy's room.

Receiving permission to enter from the nurse, Mrs. Russell, followed closely by Maud, softly opened the door and stood at the side of the wounded man.

He was sleeping.

Maud approached with her flowers and basket of fruit, and looked at the pale face of the brave fellow who had perilled his life for her safety, and was deeply impressed by the change.

Hardy had grown thin and his lips were pinched. His curly black hair was pushed carelessly back from a smooth, clear forehead, and his partially parted lips disclosed two rows of teeth which a belle might well have envied.

Maud was deeply touched.

She had seen Hardy in the flush of strength, and had known him as a driving, energetic person, to whom physical oppositions were as playthings, and now to find him weak and helpless, asleep in broad daylight, on a hospital cot, was indeed a shock.

Hardy opened his eyes.

Before him stood, with undisguised pity and sympa thy on her face, the woman of his inner adoration, to whom he would no more think of speaking tenderly than of flying, but for whom he gladly risked life, and health, and hope.

Love cannot be analyzed.

It defies rules, and ignores bounds.

Whatever is most absurd, that Love does.

That which is never prophesied, is Love's certain doing.

Grant but the "circumstances" and many "cases" would soon be altered.

Time and opportunity denied, are the obstacles tc many a love match, and the spoilers of many a happy possibility.

It may be that these young people did not then and there canvass the exact *status* of their feeling for each other.

Most probable they did not.

But, however that may be, when Maud handed Hardy the bouquet she had tastefully arranged with her own fair hands, and smilingly said: "Dear Mr. Hardy, I am *so* sorry for you, and I *do* hope you will be well very soon," it seemed to the poor fellow as if he had inhaled several gallons of oxygen, and he had suddenly been transported from the cot of his ward to a bed of roses—from the hospital to Heaven.

"Now that I've found the way, I mean to come and see you every day," said Maud; "and I'll read you to sleep if you'll let me."

If he'd let her!

The ladies remained nearly an hour at the bedside of John Hardy, giving him such gossipy information as might tend to divert his mind from himself, and then Mrs. Russell rose, saying: "Mr. Russell is expected back at half-past six, and we must go now, so as to meet him."

Hardy turned a little in his bed.

"You knew, didn't you," continued Mrs. Russell, "that Mr. Miller is quite confident that old Delaney's companion, 'little Bob' was Mr. Russell's son?"

"Yes," replied Hardy, "so Mr. Russell tells me, but until I see and hear Miller myself, I don't take much stock in that idea. I wish I was able to be out, or at all events to be up. Then I could judge for myself. Please ask Mr. Russell to see me as early as he can to-morrow. I believe I'll make an attempt to get up then, and if I can, it won't be long till I can get my hand on the wheel."

Hardy thanked Maud again and again, for the flowers and fruit, choice in themselves but radiant as evidences of her kind thoughtfulness of him, and gratefully pressing her hand, he sank back to rest, as mother and daughter bade him "good-bye."

"Handsome, isn't he?" said Maud as they stepped into their carriage.

"Yes. I always liked Hardy's looks," said her mother. "He is not only handsome but good, which is better."

As they drove to the hotel, Maud thought of all she could do for the young man who had saved her life, and who, when she began to thank him, had begged her not to say one word about it, if she wished to please him, and in her programme, Lieut. Templeton had neither place nor thought.

CHAPTER XXVI.

ON THE TRACK AT LAST.

ITH a quick, decided step, Horace Russell entered his parlor at the hotel, followed by Miller.

"Well, daughter. Here I am," said he, and hardly had he spokenw hen two pairs of arms welcomed him, and two loving mouths saluted him.

"Here's Miller" said he, when the greetings were done; "and I tell him he must dine with us. We'll have the table spread here, so that we can be by ourselves. He has a story to tell, and I wouldn't allow him to speak of it till we were all together, so that we could all enjoy it. Isn't that so, Miller? Come, mother, Mr. Miller wants to refresh himself a bit after his ride; and as for me—well, look at me, I'm nothing but dust and dirt. How's Hardy?"

The ladies bustled about as requested, and in due time the travelers were made presentable; dinner was served, the waiter dismissed and Miller proceeded to lie.

If ever a man had a hard task before him, Miller had on this occasion, for it was absolutely necessary for him to concoct a report which would drive all interest away from Robert Delaney who, he believed, *was* the son of Mr. Russell; and to lead, in some way, the mind of his employer to the conviction that the little boy brought to the West by Delaney, the builder, was the son, in order that eventually he might produce Templeton as the man grown from "little Bob."

And yet it was an easy task.

There was an anxious, eager father, looking and hoping for the desire of his heart.

And by his side were two trusting women interested for the sake of him whom they both loved better than all the world besides.

It could not be very difficult to deceive that trio.

At all events Miller was quite ready to try.

He would have given five dollars for a pipe, but as Mr. Russell did not even use a cigar, his chance for a smoke was hopeless.

In a moment, he rallied and plunged at once into his story.

"I think," said he, "we're on the right track. Indeed, I'd almost swear it. When you first came here I didn't see any very great show in the job, but I've about concluded that I was wrong. I wasn't given any very remarkable clue, as you know very well. All I had to go on was, a boy with nine toes, brought out here twenty years ago by a drunken fellow called Delaney. There ain't any Delaney, as I can find, except a Baptist preacher out here, and I know all about him, and have ever since he was born; and besides he's got ten toes, so that doesn't count. One day when I was just about discouraged, I ran across an old fellow—he's a janitor at the jail—who remembered a builder named Delaney, and said he had an idea he went to Milwaukee at least fifteen or twenty years ago. Well, I wrote over to a friend on the force, and found that there was no such person there now, but that the records of twenty years ago showed the name quite often. Then I proposed to Mr. Russell that he and I should go there. We went, and while you were being shaved, sir, I called on Billy Oake, my old chum, and together we hunted out the facts. It seems that the very Delaney you heard of in the Tombs, was sent out here by the New York authorities, and, although when he worked he was able to take care of himself, he wasn't much better than a common 'drunk.' Our folks warned him away, he went to Milwaukee. While he was there, he led the same kind of a life, but he was always very kind to a little boy he had with him. That boy might have been his child, and it might not. Nobody seemed to know. At all events he got so outrageous there, that the supervisors shipped him back to New York, and the general belief is he died there. Nothing definite is known about the boy, except that he had lost a toe from one of his feet, and took splendid care of his daddy when he was drunk."

"Poor boy," interrupted Maud.

Mr. Russell sat with his eyes wide open, but his lips were shut tight.

A thousand boys might have been in the charge of drunken men, but it was not likely that this was any but his lost or stolen son; the missing toe was confirmation strong indeed.

Miller went on.

Every word he uttered was false.

But every point made was strong for Templeton.

"Well," said he, "nothing definite could be got at about either boy, or man, except that Delaney is believed to be dead, and the boy was heard of a year or so after they went to New York, selling newspapers. The way that came about, was rather queer. That is, I suppose, it would seem so to any man in ordinary life; nothing looks queer to me. The keeper of our city prison was in New York with one of the Milwaukee officers, and this little chap was seen near the head of Wall street, with a torn cap on the back of his head, yelling out his papers like a good one. I have an idea that I can get more about that before the week is over. But, further, I learn that the boy was tracked to a coaster which went to Boston. He shipped as 'Bill' and was very sick when the vessel reached port. That's all I've got as yet, but—"

"Well, I should think that was considerable," said Mr. Russell, "for, of course, there is a regular system about such matters. If he was sick, he was taken to the hospital, and the records will tell what was done with him afterwards."

"Yes," said Miller, "and that can be ascertained just as well by letter, as in person. I propose having our Chief write to the hospital an official letter. That will fetch the answer quicker than a private letter."

"When can you see the Chief?" asked Mr. Russell.

"Well, I could see him to-night," replied Miller; "but I thought, perhaps, it would help a little if you were to go with me."

"All right," said Mr. Russell; "we'll go together in the morning. I congratulate you, Miller. I congratulate myself. I declare I begin to feel as if we were certain of success. Be here by ten in the morning, Miller. Don't fail, will you."

Miller gave the promise and retired, chuckling as he went—for he saw his way to Templeton's triumph as clearly as he saw the moon in the sky.

All he needed now was a letter from the Boston officials narrating the facts in relation to Templeton, who, it will be remembered, *was* known at the work-house as "Bill," and only assumed the name of

William Templeton, when adopted by his Massachusetts friend.

It seemed perfectly plain sailing to Miller, who had not yet been brought in contact with John Hardy, and had strangely enough forgotten that Templeton had once broached his nefarious scheme to the New York detective, and had been bluffed.

However, as matters were, he was satisfied; and, as he thought they would be, he was content.

He speedily gained his house, and after a brief chat with his daughters, went with Templeton to his room, where they sat together until long after midnight, arranging and planning for future success.

The Russells sat up late also, but all their plans were born of love, and all their projects pointed in the direction of hope and happiness, for the object of their search, in whom the heart and soul of the entire family now seemed wrapped.

CHAPTER XXVII.

THREE LITTLE BOYS—BILL, BOB, AND HARRY.

AMONG the letters on Mr. Russell's table the following day was one which attracted Maud's attention the moment she entered the room. She took it up. It was addressed to Horace Russell, Esq., but it bore no resemblance to an ordinary business letter.

She wondered what it might be.

Mr. Russell soon joined her, and she begged him to open it first of all.

He did so, and found it to be an invitation for himself and ladies, from a leading lawyer of the city, to meet a few friends at his house on the following evening.

Horace shook his head, but Maud coaxed so strenuously in favor of an acceptance that he agreed to leave it entirely to his wife. If she said "yes," he would go; otherwise, he would not.

When Mrs. Russell came in, her husband placed the invitation in her hand without a word. She read it and glanced quickly at Maud.

That settled it.

She saw that Maud wanted to go, and at once she said, "Well, father, I suppose Maud would be glad of a little change. I think we will go if you can spare the evening."

Horace laughed good-naturedly. The decision was in no sense a surprise to him.

Had Maud expressed a wish for a four-yolked egg, her parents would have secured every hen in the western country, rather than appear averse to gratifying her desire.

The evening came, and the Russells drove to the residence of their host.

The house was one of the finest in the city, the abode of culture and wealth, the favorite rendezvous of a circle of refinement and worth, where the best people of the city met and discussed and often decided plans affecting the moral and physical projects of the State.

On this occasion a rather notable gathering was assembled, and much interest was felt in the expected appearance of the millionaire Englishman with the singular mission.

Whatever may have been the opinion of the people present concerning Mr. Russell, when he entered the room with wife and daughter on either arm, there was no division of sentiment about Maud.

She was perfectly dressed and looked like a picture.

She was under, rather than above, the average height, very prettily formed, in perfect health, and flushed with happiness and anticipation.

Her beautiful hair was neither "banged," nor "frizzled," nor tortured in any way. She wore it parted in the middle of her head, brushed simply back to her comb of shell, about which it was coiled in thick and massive plaits.

Her dress was white silk, rich but plain, and her only ornaments a pair of exquisite solitaire pearl earrings and cross of pearls.

Maud knew her beauty, but it did not make her vain.

It pleased her father, and delighted her mother;—for what else had she to care?

Mrs. Russell was the recipient of much attention which she received modestly and bore in a very ladylike way, while her husband, manly outside and in, was very soon engaged in earnest conversation with several "solid men," who, like himself, were interested in the great problem of the day, and perplexed as all men are who try to solve the conundrum of Labor and Capital.

"I dare say you think," said the host of the evening, "that our system of quadrennial elections, involving frequent change of administration, has something to do with what you call our 'unsettlement,' Mr. Russell."

"Yes, I do, most certainly," answered the Englishman; "it stands to reason that officials who are kept in place only by favor of party, cannot give their entire time, thought and energy to their duty. And without that devotion to duty, no official can be competent. With us a good clerk in the postal or customs service is certain of his position for life. Here he hardly gets warm in his seat before he has to make room for another."

"I grant you there is something in that," rejoined the gentleman, "but I was referring more especially to the President."

"Well," said Mr. Russell, "you would hardly expect an Englishman to agree with the accepted American theory that constant change is as beneficial as permanence and solidity. I know you argue that the President always exists, and only the individual changes. But I do not think facts warrant the assertion—when your 'man' changes, your whole government changes, from cabinet officers to customs searchers. We, on the outside, as friendly critics, see better than you do, if you will permit me, a gradual tendency to centralization, which we believe will in the end be of inestimable benefit to this nation.

And, unless I greatly misjudge your people, these con stantly recurring excitements are more and more dis tasteful year after year."

"You refer to the election excitements?"

"Yes. You elected President Lincoln twice, and it was often remarked at home that his re-election was but the entering wedge. His third election was quite probable; his death removed the test. But you re-elected President Grant, and——"

"Oh, Mr. Russell," broke in a jolly-faced party, who had held a prominent judicial seat since his early manhood, and was as full of fun as he was of experience, "that won't do. No third-term talk here to-night; you'll drive our Chicago friends wild if you start on that."

"Oh, no, he won't," chimed in the host; "Mr. Russell is evidently a Grant man. Let's hear the rest of your sentence, Mr. Russell. You were saying that we had re-elected Grant."

"Yes," said Mr. Russell; "I was simply showing that although President Lincoln's death precluded the solution of the problem in his case, you had at the very first opportunity re-elected a president, and now, as the next general election draws near, I find a decided feeling in favor of continuing the incumbent a third time, and why not a fourth and a fifth?"

"Which of course you think would be a good idea?"

"Certainly it would. Not that this or that man is necessarily the best to be found for the position, but being there he retains subordinates who are familiar with their duty, and who are sure to be removed if a new chief is elected."

"Well, as the judge says, this third-term discussion is apt to be a long one," said the gentleman of the house; "but it is certainly full of interest, especially if not discussed for or against any special person."

"Certainly," said Mr. Russell; "I was arguing for the principle, not at all in the interest of any individual. We think from what we see and read, that President Grant, however, has a tremendous leverage. His sixty thousand office-holders are a great power. He ought to be able to control the convention, and doubtless his name is still potent with thousands of voters in the country, where all memories of the 'bloody chasm' are not yet forgotten, and where the 'red flag' argument is still very powerful. And then the capitalists must dread change. It really seems to me, you know, that if the present president were to use his power, he could do pretty much as he pleased."

Mrs. Russell had been leaning upon the arm of her host during this conversation, and several ladies had joined the group, evidently interested in the turn the discussion had taken. As Mr. Russell closed his last sentence, a young gentleman entered the room, and approaching the lady of the house, saluted her and her husband. After a moment's conversation he was turning away, when the lady said:

"Mr. Delaney, let me present you to Mrs. Russell of England, and Mr. Russell also."

Horace started, looked quickly at the handsome face and sturdy figure, and then grasped the young clergyman's hand with marked and noticeable interest.

Opportunity was not afforded at the moment, but, in the course of the evening, Mr. Russell asked his host "what he knew about Mr. Delaney?"

He replied that he was a very popular and much respected preacher of their city, a native and life-long resident of Chicago, and a man not only of great force, but of great goodness of character as well.

Mr. Russell brushed away from his imagination the dim outlines of a picture there forming, but he could not efface the impression the young man had made upon his mind.

As he looked about the spacious apartment, he saw Maud and the young clergyman in conversation.

Excusing himself, he approached them as Maud said: "I should be very happy to go, I assure you, and if you can call at the hotel, both papa and mamma will be pleased to see you."

"Yes, indeed, we will, Mr. Delaney," said Mr. Russell; "we shall doubtless be here three or four weeks longer, and if you can spare the time, we'll be heartily glad to see you. Where is it you want Maud to go?"

"I had been telling her of my new church, sir," replied Mr. Delaney; "and of what we consider a delightful feature—an admirable choir, with a superb organ, and your daughter was kind enough to say she should be pleased to go to the church."

"Of course she would," said Mr. Russell; "of course she would—and so would Mrs. Russell and myself. We'll go next Sunday. Why can't you dine with us on Sunday? Oh, I beg pardon; perhaps Mrs. Delaney——"

Mr. Delaney laughed. "You need have no fear of that good woman, Mr. Russell. As yet she exists only in imagination, and is as manageable as she is ethereal. I was trying to recall whether I had an engagement to dine at Mr. Miller's on Sunday. I think I have."

Mr. Delaney was a clergyman, to be sure, but clergymen are men, and men are apt to remember their engagements with the darlings of their hearts.

It was the young preacher's custom, now, to dine every Sunday at Mr. Miller's.

On that day One-eyed Charley was rarely at home, as the dinner hour was at one instead of six o'clock, as usual. Not that he would have objected to Mr. Delaney's visits. On the contrary, he liked the man, and, possibly, if he had kept his eye about him, he would have seen, what everybody else saw, that the clergyman was desperately in love with the pretty Martha

And if he *had* seen that, would he have done his best to keep Delaney and Russell apart, or would he have kicked Templeton's dirty money into the street, and bade the schemer and his nine toes depart?

It was finally arranged that Mr. Russell would take his wife and daughter to Mr. Delaney's church the following Sunday, and they all looked forward to the time with pleasure.

The evening passed agreeably.

Maud was a favorite at once. She danced gracefully and was very fond of it. Her hand was in constant requisition, and she enjoyed an exceedingly happy time.

Mrs. Russell was well cared for, and Horace was the lion of the occasion. Every one knew that he was a man of mark among his fellows at home, that he represented very large commercial interests, and that he was at present engaged in a search as romantic as it was creditable. He was not a brilliant man, but he had hard common sense, and like all sensible men, he made himself felt wherever he went.

It was quite late when Mr. Russell's carriage was announced; then bidding his friends "good night," the good man with his wife and daughter returned to their hotel.

There they found Miller.

Without a moment's delay, Miller took Mr. Russell by the arm, and leading him toward the window, said: "Mr. Russell, keep calm, sir; I believe we have a clue to your son. The Chief has received a letter from Boston, which says they have ascertained that *a* boy called 'Bill' was either adopted by a gentleman or bound out to a harness-maker, at the time referred to, and they will spare no pains to ascertain the *facts*, and when we get them, the game is done."

It would be idle to attempt to paint the delight and joy of Horace Russell and his wife and daughter.

"Truly," said he, "my cup runneth over."

CHAPTER XXVIII.

THE SNAKE FASCINATES MARY MILLER.

IN conversation with Templeton, Miller had so thoroughly convinced him that their deception would succeed in the end, that all thought of marrying Maud had been driven from his mind.

So far as Templeton knew, Maud was Mr. Russell's own daughter. Marriage with her was, to him, obviously impossible in the event of Mr. Russell's accepting him as his long-lost son. And, beside, Templeton had found in Mary Miller a much more congenial companion.

It was now nearly three months since he was first introduced to the Miller home.

A large part of that time he had been forced into the society of Miller's daughters, and as Martha was devoted to the humanitarian duties assigned her by her pastor, Templeton had no choice in the matter—he remained with Mary.

Mary Miller was a good girl.

She loved her sister and idolized her father.

Outside of the church circle she had but few acquaintances and no near friends.

The society of gentlemen was unknown to her. What wonder, then, that she became interested in this young friend of her father, who added to graces of person, the charms of culture and the polish gained by travel?

They read and talked together. She sang to him, and he told her of all he had seen at home and abroad.

Insensibly she passed from interest to regard, and thence to love.

In her eyes Templeton was a hero.

No romance ever painted serener beauty than his. No fairy ever wove more exquisite garments than those in which Mary Miller's fancy invested her lover.

And he—well, he did not love her, for love was a feeling whose depths he never sounded, but he liked her, and was pleased at her attentions.

Intentionally he never led her a step, but, for all that, the steps were taken, and, before he really suspected it, Templeton found himself the girl's idol, her all in all, the one thing needful for her heart's comfort and the delight of her soul.

Man-like he did nothing to stop it.

He simply shrugged his shoulders and let her love him.

When he one day was left by her for a few moments, Miller being about his duties, out of town, and Martha on her circuit, Templeton looked the matter squarely in the face. "If I permit this girl's love for me to be known to her father, will it help or mar my plans? Will Miller consent to her marriage with a man he does not trust? And if not, what becomes of her? If, again, I marry her unknown to her father, am I not in position to turn his flank when occasion requires, and, through his love for his daughter, hold him to any bargain and any secret, whether he like it or not?"

Thus pondering, Templeton slowly walked the floor, supporting himself a little with his cane; for although his foot had entirely healed, there was still a sensitiveness about it when pressed, that induced him to favor it in walking.

The right or wrong of his conduct in no way trouble or influenced Templeton.

All he cared for was success.

That, he believed, would certainly be assured through Miller, in whom he had implicit confidence; but into Miller's hands he did not care to trust everything—and because of that unwillingness, he deliberately concluded to retain the affections of the detective's daughter, and be guided by his necessities, when the question of matrimony arose.

Presently, Mary returned, and said: "Oh, Mr. Russell, here is some new music we have just received; wouldn't you like to come down stairs and hear me try it? It's an arrangement of Aïda, and they say it is perfectly charming."

Templeton acquiesced, and together they went to the parlor, but it was some time before the piano was opened, for, drawing Mary to a seat, the curious fellow said: "Mary, we have been thrown very strangely together. Why, of course, you do not know, nor is it necessary that you should. Suffice it that being here, a happy fate has made me almost your constant companion. Before my accident, you were kindness itself, but during the two weeks of my confinement to my room, had you been my own sister, or my lover, I could not have asked or looked for more attentive courtesy and help."

"Oh, Mr. Russell, surely I did nothing more than was natural," said Mary.

"That I grant," continued Templeton; "and the fact that it was so natural, is all the more creditable to you, and perhaps more complimentary to me. I find our tastes are similar. You are fond of reading, and on your shelves are the books I prize the most. You are devoted to music, and how our likes and dislikes in that direction harmonize, you know very well. On the whole, I think we are tolerably good friends, Mary, and why not more than good friends? Why not the *best* of friends?"

Templeton had gone further than he intended.

Had he been talking to a woman of the world, he might have continued in that strain indefinitely, satisfying himself and amusing her.

Had he been practicing his arts upon a flirt, he might have met his match in retort and repartee.

But Mary was neither one nor the other.

She was a genuine woman.

To her a spade was a spade.

She had no lovers. Her father and Mr. Delaney were the only men she had ever known intimately. Her only outside life had been in the school-room. She was but eighteen years old. She never lied. She knew nothing of the world, its tricks, or its manners She believed what she heard, and invariably said precisely what she meant.

She loved Templeton.

To be sure, he had never uttered a syllable which could be construed into a declaration or an invitation.

But she loved him.

And now that he had, with tender accent, respectfully, courteously and with apparent sincerity, asked if she knew any reason why they should not be the "*best* of friends," it seemed as if her dream of happiness had been realized.

Turning quickly to him, Mary looked her lover full in the eye, with unmistakable meaning, and then as he pressed her closely to his heart, she whispered her consent.

If there *is* a Devil, how happy such scenes must make him!

CHAPTER XXIX.

ON THE ROCKS.

OOR Hardy!

How he chafed, and rolled, and tumbled, in his bed!

The days were years, the weeks were ages. It seemed to him as if his life was a blank, and he a cipher.

That is, it seemed so until Maud Russell's daily visits made his life a holiday, and his experience an intoxication.

Probably many may regard Maud's every-day call with disfavor.

That is their privilege.

The fact is, she did go every day in every week, carrying flowers and fruits, and books and cheeriness of angelic type, making the sick chamber radiant with joy, and the sick man a convalescent speedily.

Of all the men here told of, John Hardy was most liked by Horace Russell.

He was a fine specimen of manhood—tall, straight and strong.

His features were regular, but not feminine. His eye and lip showed courage, and his manner, though not offensive, was aggressive rather than quiet.

Mr. Russell had "taken to" him at the very first, and every interview increased his respect and esteem for him. He found him earnest, intelligent and truthful, and when, in a moment, the young man was reduced to a scarcely breathing mass of flesh and bones, the strong Englishman felt as if part of himself had been broken away.

With Maud, Hardy had been thrown but very little until the trip westward.

She had seen him every day at the hotel in New York, and he had been one of the party of four on their excursions in and about the city; still, until the memorable ride, which ended in disaster, Maud had really felt but little interest in the young man, on whose skill and service so much of her father's future happiness depended.

Love of romance has a strong hold on a young girl's mind.

Of late Hardy had seemed to Maud like a character in fiction, rather than a being of ordinary type.

His personal history had interested her, as it had her parents. His chivalrous endeavor to preserve her life, and shield her person, inspired her with gratitude

His suffering and long confinement excited her sympathy. And now that he was slowly gaining, being permitted to sit in his chair several hours every day, his pale face and lustrous eyes, and evident delight at her attention, elicited an interest which strengthened at every interview.

Mrs. Russell and Maud always called together, but on several occasions Maud remained, while her mother drove elsewhere, and read to Hardy the news of the day, or from such current literature as she thought would divert his mind.

Insensibly they became well acquainted and thoroughly at home in each other's presence.

Hardy was one of Nature's gentlemen—a much better article than that of the world, although not so good a dancer.

He would have died rather than say or do aught that could offend Maud Russell, and yet he loved her with all his heart, and worshipped her very shadow.

While she was with him, he was in heaven; and when she was gone, he counted the hours till she should return.

By day, he thought of her; by night, he dreamed of her.

And why not?

What insurmountable difference was there between them?

Money!

Nothing but money!

Not that John Hardy sneered at money. No sensible person does that. Money is a good friend, though a bad master. What a good man can do with money can never be exaggerated. And the good men who insist that money is nothing to them, and proclaim that they are happier without it than they would be with it, are either liars or fools.

The world never yet saw the sane man who would not gladly take all the money he could honestly get.

One might as well decline to use his brains, or his hands, or his feet, or any other useful convenience, as to ridicule the usefulness and desirability of money—and the more the better.

Still, as between John Hardy and Maud Russell, money was the only embarrassment.

Maud had none, but her father had millions.

"Suppose," thought Hardy, in one of his ten thousand dreams; "suppose I could win Maud's heart, how could I gain her hand? I know her parents like me, but would they consent? These English people think so much of social position, and I am only a detective, the son of a scavenger!"

Poor Hardy!

Over and over again, he thought and thought the same old story, and it always ended the same way. He could not seem to bring it to any other close. "I am only a detective, the son of a scavenger."

One day Maud came alone.

Hardy was sitting up as usual, and had been felicitating himself on the progress which enabled him, for the first time that morning, to walk unaided from his bedside to the adjoining room, when Maud Russell entered.

Something had happened.

The girl was bewilderingly beautiful.

Her eyes were half filled with tears, and fairly bright with excitement.

Without stopping for explanation or query as to Hardy's condition, Maud broke out: "Oh, Mr. Hardy, *what* do you think, what *do* you think we've found? There's no doubt about it. Mr. Miller says so, and father says so, and father's almost wild with he doesn't know what;" and bursting into tears, the excited girl sat down, sobbing from the bottom of her heart.

Hardy was alarmed.

He had always seen Maud so quiet and composed, so perfect in deportment, so self-poised and gentle in her bearing, that this flood of passion disconcerted him.

His experience should have taught him that a calm and placid exterior is rarely an exponent of a womanly interior.

All he did or said was: "Why, what's the matter?"

"A great deal's the matter," replied Maud, who threw back her veil, wiped her eyes, arranged her hat by the glass, and continuing, said: "You know papa and that horrid Miller have been trying to find that 'little Bob,' that ma and I never *have* believed in, and they've been writing to Boston—but you know all about that, for papa told you. Well, they've found *who* he is, but they don't know *where* he is. And who *do* you think he is? The last man on the face of the earth that anybody would have *dreamed* of. Guess."

"Why, bless your heart, I never could guess. I might guess one man as well as another," said Hardy.

"Well, it's Mr. Lieutenant William Templeton," cried Maud, springing to her feet; "*that's* who it is. Now, what do you think of that?"

John Hardy looked like a ghost. He was as pale as a sheet, and about as stiff. Two thoughts presented themselves at once:

Either Templeton was an infamous and a successful scoundrel;

Or, he was sincere and in earnest when he told Hardy that he was Russell's son, and wanted Hardy to help him prove it.

If the former were the fact, how could Hardy bluff him?

If the latter, farewell to all hope of happiness with Maud.

"Well, what do you mean by saying your father is almost wild?" asked Hardy, at last.

"Why, father *hates* Templeton. The very sight of the man used to make him cross and ugly. He forbade us to speak to him. He actually *hated* him, and now to find out that he is his *own son;* that they have been rude to each other; that—oh, I don't know; it does seem to me as if everything and everybody was mad and out of sorts. Papa will be here, by and by. Mamma told me to drive down, and to tell you to be just as cool and calm as you can be; for papa is dreadfully excited. And he trusts that old Miller almost as much as he does you; but we don't. Mamma and I *never* liked him. He rolls that wicked old eye all over the wall, and never looks at anybody. I *hate* him. But you'll be cool, won't you?"

Hardy laughed in spite of himself.

It seemed to him that Maud's endeavors to keep him cool, were very much like the effort made to keep powder safe, by stirring it with a red hot poker.

He had no time to reply before the door opened, and Mr. and Mrs. Russell entered.

Horace Russell was getting on towards his fifty-fifth year, but he felt as if he were in his prime.

He enjoyed perfect health, and this long rest from active and constant business life was doing him an immensity of good.

He was handsome as a picture.

His head was bald, but his eye was strong and clear. No beard obscured the perfect lines of face and mouth, and chin. His body was erect and stalwart, and every action told of the manhood of the man.

Although greatly excited, his strong common sense controlled an exhibition of his feeling. Taking Hardy by the hand, he said: "My dear boy, you cannot know, you never can, how perfectly delighted I am at your progress. I thank God, day and night, for it. You look better, you are better, and the doctor tells me we can have you with us at the hotel next Sunday. Much as I want, yes, much as I need you, you know I am most glad for your own sake. Doesn't he look bright to-day, mother?"

Maud and Hardy were deceived, but Mrs. Russell was not.

She knew that her husband meant every word he said.

But she also knew that his heart was crushed, and his soul in agony at the news brought that morning by Miller's eastern mail.

Sweetly smiling, Mrs. Russell, who was the embodiment of all good old-fashioned ideas of motherliness, took Hardy's hand in hers, and turning to her husband, said: "Mr. Hardy is doing so well, dear, that he will forgive you for being selfish to-day. Sit down and tell him just how you feel, and what you have heard."

"I see Maud has told you the news," said Mr. Russell.

"Only a little, papa," said Maude. "You would better commence at the beginning and tell him all."

Mrs. Russell handed her husband a chair, and he proceeded with his report.

"I told you that Miller had heard from the Boston people the bare fact of 'Bob' Delaney's leaving the workhouse hospital, and being adopted by some unknown party, didn't I?"

"Yes, sir," said Hardy; "that was the last I heard."

"Well, I told Miller to send $100 to his friend, and direct him to follow that clue. He did so, and last night Miller received this letter, which he brought to me this morning. I'll read it to you, if I can, for I declare, it has almost taken my pluck and strength away. I'll tell you why afterwards. Here, mother, you read it. Oh, you haven't brought your glasses. Daughter, you read it, I—upon my word, I dislike even to look at it."

Maud read the letter as follows, and Hardy listened as if to a choir of angels:

BOSTON, *October 22d*, 1874.

MR. CHARLES MILLER,
Police headquarters, Chicago.

"SIR—Your favor of the 18th was duly received,

and requests noted. I am pleased to reply that with out much trouble I can satisfy your bill of inquiry. It seems that the boy 'Bob' was entered on the books as 'Bill,' and when taken to the hospital that was all the name he had. I was in some doubt as to his being the boy, but I have found a sister of the man who adopted him, a maiden lady living in Chelsea, who satisfied me on that point. She went with her brother to see the boy while he was sick, and when her brother brought him home, she heard him ask the boy whether he preferred to be called by his old name or take a new one. And she tells how pleased her brother was when the little chap said: 'I'll take your name if you'll let me.' So I am confident on that point. The rest is simple. The boy was thenceforth known as William Templeton. He went into the navy, and now he is a lieutenant in the service.

"If I can be of any further use, command me, and it shall be done. Respectfully,

"JAMES HOWES,
"State Constabulary."

"What do you think of that?" sai Mr. Russell.

"Where is Templeton?" said Hardy, without noticing the question.

"We don't know," replied Mr. Russell. "He left New York very suddenly, and has never been heard of since."

"Does Miller know him?"

"I think not; he said he must try to hunt him up."

"The doctor says I can go out on Sunday, does he?" said Hardy. "Well, that's day after to-morrow. I think, when I join you at the hotel, I must meet Miller. You know he has never seen me. I'll meet him in your parlors as an English friend just arrived, and perhaps I can judge him better there than I could if he were on his guard against a fellow officer. Meanwhile, let him talk and plan, and report. It may be he is perfectly honest, and Templeton is your son; it may not be. I *feel* that there is some trickery, but——"

"Oh, my God," said Mr. Russell. "I thank you, Hardy. Much as I love my boy, much as I long, yes, hunger for him, I cannot believe that man to be my son. Hardy, my boy, I won't insult you by talking of money. I trust you, my dear fellow, absolutely. We all do. Mother will tell you how perfectly I trust you. Now, don't let me weary you, but for Heaven's sake put your wits to work. If there is any trickery here, let's have it out. If not—well, Heaven's will, not mine, be done."

Hardy grasped the poor man by the hand, but he could not speak.

He saw the grief and the wreck, but he dared not tell his suspicions.

If Templeton really were the son, it would only make matters worse to expose his meanness and craft.

If he were not the son, time and circumstances would doubtless establish the fact.

But Miller was now in Hardy's mind.

And, sharp and shrewd, and hard as Miller undeniably was, it was a bad place for Miller to be.

CHAPTER XXX.

MILLER DOES SOME TALKING.

ACT is often quite as strange as fiction, and odd as it may seem, although the Russells had been several times to hear Mr. Delaney preach, and, on one occasion, the young clergyman had passed an evening with the ladies—Mr. Russell having an engagement elsewhere—the fact that his name was "Robert" had never been made known.

Indeed, if it had been, it is doubtful if they would have thought anything of it, for their confidence in Miller had not been shaken, although Maud disliked him from the first.

And yet the simple fact remained that Mr. Russell was spending money like water, hoping to find a "Bob" Delaney, and was now confronted with one who had changed his name to "William Templeton," while in his own parlor his wife and daughter were entertaining *the* "Bob" of his search.

Of this Miller had satisfied himself beyond a doubt.

He knew perfectly well that old Delaney, the builder, the "father" of Robert Delaney, had never returned to New York; that he had never left Chicago at all. He knew when and how he died; and he knew the young man at whose church his daughter attended, and who visited at his house, was the identical "Bob" for whom his employer searched.

As yet he did *not* know that he was also the son whom Mr. Russell lost.

But he was in dread of such a revelation, and feared every day of his life that some accident would confirm his suspicions.

Neither did he know that Mr. Russell had met Mr. Delaney, much less that the clergyman was an occasional caller at his rooms.

Judge then, his surprise, when, on Saturday afternoon, prior to the anticipated Sunday of Hardy's emancipation, Miller came face to face with Mr. Russell and Mr. Delaney in the corridor of the hotel.

Mr. Delaney's greeting was cordial and straightforward, but it was really a test of Miller's admirable training. He controlled himself perfectly, and when Mr. Russell said: "Ah, you know, Mr. Miller, do you, Mr. Delaney?" both men smiled, and with some affirmatory remark, the three passed up stairs to Mr. Russell's rooms.

"Anything new, Miller?" asked Mr. Russell.

"Yes, a little," said the detective. "I find that

our bird took passage for Nassau about the time you say he left New York. His resignation from the service was dated the day before he sailed. I have sent a letter, or rather the Chief has, to the consul there, with instructions upon two points only. They are, first: 'Has Templeton lost a little toe?' and second, 'When is he coming back to the United States?'"

"Very important that," broke in Mr. Russell; "I declare, Miller, you give me new life. That man never lost a toe; I know he never did. His walk was perfect. Bless my soul! do you know I never thought of that? Of course he never lost a toe."

"But, my dear sir," said Miller, "what am I to understand? Do you want to find your man or don't you?"

Mr. Russell looked at Miller sharply.

He remembered what Hardy had said, and here at the very first interview, he was disclosing to Miller his feelings and his fears.

"Why should I distrust this man?" thought he. "He is recommended to me by his chief. He stands at the head of his fellows. He has been kind and industrious. I pay him well. What can he gain by being false. What will he not gain, if successful? I'll tell him all."

Thus resolving, Mr. Russell drew Miller away from the group, and putting his honest hand on the old rascal's shoulder, said: "Miller, I know this man

Templeton. He was a fellow-passenger of ours. I disliked him exceedingly. He was attentive to my daughter, and although that is generally an open door to a father's heart, I disliked him all the more. And besides, I am not Maud's father. She was Mrs. Russell's child by a former husband."

Miller's red hair wanted to stand up, but Miller's detective nerve kept his red hair down.

"Not his daughter," thought he; "what then might become of Mary, his own daughter, whose affections he saw plainly were twined and interlaced with Templeton's very life. If Templeton could be proved Mr. Russell's son—he thought—of course he could not marry Russell's daughter: and if he married Miller's daughter, there was another bond between the father and the conspirator." But this revelation opened a way by which Templeton might play Miller false.

Once let it be shown that Templeton was Russell's son, and that Maud was not Russell's daughter, what could bar their marriage?

Meanwhile Mr. Russell, all unconscious of the hubbub he had caused in Miller's mind, proceeded:

"She was Mrs. Russell's child by a former husband, but I love her as my own. She was passionately fond of Lieut. Templeton, but I would not permit her to see him. After the fire, the dear child seemed to droop, and reluctantly we consented that Templeton should call. A note was sent inviting him to do so, but it was unanswered. He never sent a word of apology or regret, or explanation; and I had hoped we should never hear his cursed name again. Judge then, Miller, how utterly unprepared I was for such an astounding revelation as yours. I *feel* that there is no truth in it. And yet—do not misunderstand me, I do not doubt *you*—the trace seems clear, and I see that your mind is settled—"

"Hold on, Mr. Russell," said Miller, with well assumed warmth; "if you were to say to me, 'Miller, I don't want this followed up,' that would end it. But don't make any mistake. I'm by no manner of means *settled* in my mind. No, sir. What I want is, first of all, to see that toe! Or, rather *not* to see that toe. And after that I want to see the rest of him. I think we must both own up that the clue so far is a strong one. But suppose he has never lost a toe—that *settles* it, doesn't it? Well, then. But if, on the other hand, his toe is gone, we must admit again that the clue is all the stronger. And then if, on acquaintance and careful examination, we find he *is* the boy, why it seems to me, as honest men, we must say so.

"If you don't like the fellow you needn't have anything to do with him. He can't prove himself your son, unless you help him, can he? Well, then. Now you just leave this to me. If you don't want another step taken, the job stops right here. If you do, on it goes. Very much depends on the toe, and after all he may be a nicer fellow than you thought."

Mr. Russell was impressed by Miller's manner, and had it not been for a recollection of John Hardy's advice, would very likely have yielded then and there. As it was, he simply said: "Come and see me to-morrow evening. I'll think it all over, and by that time we will come to some conclusion."

Miller bowed himself out without much formality, and Mr. Russell turned to Mr. Delaney, who, with the ladies, was looking at the sunset from the window.

"That's a queer character, Mr. Delaney," said Mr. Russell.

"Oh, Miller? Yes, indeed. I can never make out whether he is in fun or in earnest," said Mr. Delaney; "his daughters attend my church and are among my warmest friends. I have visited at the house a great deal, though I see but little of the father. He is certainly a very strange man to have such charming daughters. One of them, by the way, is betrothed to a gentleman of your name, Mr. Russell."

"Do you know him?" asked Maud.

"No. I have never met him, but he is well spoken of, naturally, by the young ladies, and I judge, from all I hear, he is quite accomplished. He lives in New York, I believe; but really I don't know anything about it."

"It seems strange that Miller should have two daughters and never allude to them," said Maud.

"Oh, I don't know," said her father; "we have had nothing to do with him outside of business; although, come to think of it, all the time we were in Milwaukee he received no letters, and never spoke of home at all."

"I suppose men in his position sink their individuality in their business," suggested the clergyman.

"Yes, and they are naturally chary of their confidence," said Mr. Russell; "but I have met one officer of whose friendship and regard I shall always be proud. When we left New York, a Detective named Hardy, John Hardy, was assigned to aid me in my search, and, as doubtless you remember, he was very seriously injured in the accident from which we so providentially escaped. I think I never met an officer more cool, more prudent, more clear-headed; and he has absolutely devoted himself to our service. He nas won my heart completely, and as for mother here, she thinks there never was such a man."

"Oh, father, that's rather strong," said Mrs. Russell; "but we certainly have cause to be grateful to Mr. Hardy, and, as Mr. Russell says, he seems honesty and goodness itself."

"I'm sure *I* like him," said Maud; "I always did like him. He was so respectful and kind to papa, and then he saved my life, you know, Mr. Delaney; and——"

"And so you chant his praises," laughingly said Mr. Delaney; "that is right, perfectly right. And where is Mr. Hardy?"

"He is still at the hospital," said Mr. Russell; "but he will be here to-morrow, and before we leave town, I hope you will meet him. You will take to each other, I know."

In some way the conversation turned. Mr. Russell and his wife, anxious and ill at ease about Templeton, while Maud and Mr. Delaney, after talking about some new music Maud had bought, went to the piano, where, for a long time, the petted girl entertained the visitor, and cheered the sorrowing hearts of her troubled parents.

How or why, we never know and can never explain, but, at times, that which on other occasions would seem offensive and intrusive, becomes most natural and welcome.

And so it was that Mr. Delaney, who felt, without knowing, that something had disturbed the comfort of his hosts, cemented the regard already existing as a bond between his new friends and himself, by saying: "Before I go, let us ask the direction and blessing of our Father," and, kneeling at his chair, he uttered a tender, honest petition for protection, guidance and forgiveness, to which, with one accord, they said: "Amen."

CHAPTER XXXI.

BEWARE, POOR GIRL; BEWARE.

WHEN Miller left Mr. Russell's hotel he pulled his hat hard and far down over his eye.

Every word he had told his employer was false.

It had not been received as he had hoped.

Templeton had, indeed, informed him of Mr. Russell's dislike, but Miller had detected a much deeper feeling than simple dislike.

He saw that the very name of Templeton was distasteful to the entire family, and that Maud, instead of hailing the news with joy and hope, shared her father's annoyance and repugnance.

And then, too, Delaney's presence troubled the detective.

"How came he there? What is he there for? Is it possible that other trails are being followed?" These and kindred queries thrust themselves upon Miller's perplexed mind, and insisted upon solution.

Since undertaking this search, Miller had not touched a drop of liquor. Now and then he took a pint of ale or a glass of beer, but nothing stronger. He had deliberately chosen Templeton as against Russell, and having laid out his programme, pursued it with absolute loyalty. He had given time and money and thought to the prosecution of his plan. He had kept Templeton at his own house, had compelled him to sacrifice his toe, had gone off on long trips, apparently on Mr. Russell's business, but in reality to further Mr. Russell's deception, and had gradually worked up his case so that it was now susceptible almost of exact demonstration that Templeton, little "Bob," and the lost Harry Russell were one and the same person.

Miller had done all this, but with a detective's intuition he felt that something was wrong.

Whether it was Delaney or Templeton upon whom his plan would wreck, he could not determine.

In his heart he believed Robert Delaney was Mr. Russell's son.

He had devoted days to the investigation, and had clearly proven to himself that the clergyman was not the son of the old builder, that he was the boy who was sent with Delaney from the Tombs, and that he was lame.

But the toe?

Miller had done his best to ascertain if Mr. Delaney had lost a toe, but without success. He had ingeniously pumped his bootmaker and tailor. He had talked with the men who were in Delaney's regiment. He had followed him for hours in the streets.

And he was as ignorant now as at the first.

Dreading the possibilities of confidence between Mr. Russell and his new friend, Miller determined to bring the Templeton development to an immediate issue, and went directly home.

He found Templeton sitting with Mary in the dimly lighted parlor and greeted them both cheerily.

His daughter welcomed him with a loving embrace, and hastened to order dinner.

Templeton and Miller were alone together.

The old man placed one hand on the knee of the handsome youth beside him, and said very quietly: "No nonsense, young man; no nonsense *there*. If you don't love that girl, don't pretend to."

Templeton colored up and began to speak, but Miller interrupted him and simply said: "There now, that'll do, I know you pretty well, and you know me. All I say is, no nonsense; and that ends it. After dinner I want to see you alone. You propose a walk or a game of back-gammon up-stairs, and whatever you say, I'll agree to."

Templeton saw that Miller meant all he said, and inwardly resolved to back out of his pleasantry with Mary before the father's ire had good cause to rise.

And poor Mary? Oh! he didn't think of her at all. He cared for Templeton, not for Mary.

At the dinner table sat two scoundrels and two innocents. The scoundrels were quiet and thoughtful. So were the innocents.

Miller was completing his plans.

Templeton was seeking a way out of his social embarrassment.

Martha had received a long, loving letter from Mr. Delaney, and was expecting a call from him in the morning.

And Mary's heart was filled with love and admiration for the only man she had ever really known, and for whom she was willing to give up all else that made home happy and life endurable.

Each was so occupied that the other's occupation was not noticed, until Miller saw the absurdity of a Quaker meeting then and there, and twinkling his eye at Martha, said: "Well, baby, how goes our parish? Anybody dead, anybody born?"

Quick to appreciate her father's intent, Martha laughed and said: "Oh, yes. And we are to give Mr. Delaney a house-warming on Monday night. He goes into the parsonage to-day, and the church people have arranged a surprise party there on Monday night. I want you to go with us, Mr. Russell, won't you?"

"He would if he could, I have no doubt," said Miller; "but he won't be in town on Monday."

As he spoke Miller pressed Templeton's foot under the table, and taking the hint, he said: "I am really very sorry. I would go with pleasure. But, as your father says, I shall probably be away. I don't doubt you will have a jolly time. But be careful. Don't monopolize the pastor. You'll make all the others jealous if you do."

Templeton uttered his protest jokingly, but he unwittingly hit a nail squarely on the head.

Mr. Delaney's respect for Martha Miller had grown into friendship, thence to regard, and finally to unspoken love.

His attentions attracted observation and remark, until it was necessary for him to stop or go on.

He preferred to go on, and to that end wrote his fair parishioner a letter, in which he in a very manly and characteristic way laid his circumstances and plans before her, told her that he loved her and asked her to be his wife, promising to call early the next day for an answer.

Martha had, of course, told her sister of Mr. Delaney's proposal, but had as yet found no opportunity of speaking to her father. Her heart had answered "yes" almost before the question had been put in form, and she knew her father so well, that his acquiescence in aught that could contribute to her happiness was sure to be given.

Rising from her chair Martha went to her father

and placing her arm about his neck, kissed him tenderly on the forehead. "I want to see you alone, papa," she whispered, and with another kiss left the room.

As Miller prepared to follow his daughter, Templeton said : "I haven't been out of the house to-day, Mr. Miller ; what do you say to a little tramp down to the lake. Can you spare the time ?"

"Yes, of course I can. Wait till I speak with Martha a moment. Then I'll take a pipe and join you," said Miller, and off he went.

Templeton and Mary were left to themselves and withdrew to the parlor, where Mary took her seat at the piano and sang.

Her voice was very sweet and true.

She was especially fond of singing "The Wanderer," and Templeton was especially fond of hearing it.

He rather liked the girl.

She was pretty, graceful, good.

She made no concealment of her regard for him, and he knew he had but to say the word, and she would go or stay, fly to the end of the world with him or wait his time for an honorable and happy union.

But that word he had never spoken.

And Miller's warning had convinced him that to speak it and not mean it, would involve him in a quarrel with a man who would butcher him as readily and unconcernedly as he would an ox. So he determined not to speak it.

And the poor girl gave her heart to a man who not only did not want it, but was afraid to take it.

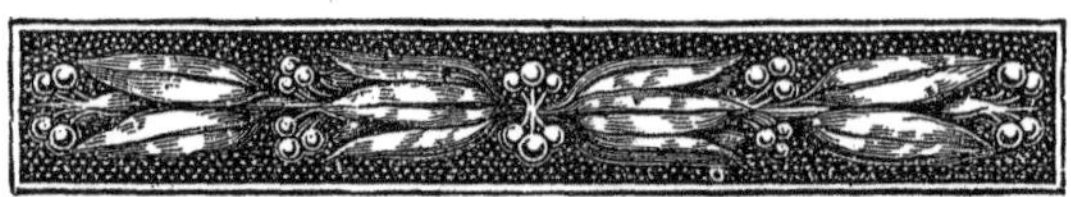

CHAPTER XXXII.

FOREWARNED FOREARMED.

ILLER rejoined Templeton after half an hour's absence and together they walked towards the lake. Miller puffed vigorously at his pipe, but did not speak. And Templeton, who was greatly embarrassed by his equivocal position with Mary, limped very gingerly, as he blew great smoky rings from underneath his long moustache.

Martha had shown Mr. Delaney's letter to her father and read it to him as she sat upon his knee.

The old fellow had a soft heart for his children and he assented at once to her desire.

But what a vision rose up before him.

His own daughter cheated by himself!

Her husband, the real Harry Russell, swindled out of home and property and love by the rascality of her own father!

A liar and pretender seated in the chair which of right belongs to Martha's husband! and he the instrument by which the infamy was done!

Even Miller was disconcerted. He had no fear of Templeton, but he had given his mind to accomplish a certain end,—had taken pay for it. He was not responsible for the curious combination of circumstances attending the case. But——

Oh, those "buts."

"What shall I do?" thought Miller.

"Martha loves and will marry Mr. Delaney. It is only necessary now, to complete the extraordinary drama, for Mary to love and marry Templeton.

"Sooner or later it will all come out.

"Well, what if it does?

"The girls love each other and the lucky one will take care of the other."

But the more Miller thought, the more complicated matters became.

The entanglements seemed endless.

He could get no aid from Templeton. He had tried him before. Whatever Miller suggested, Templeton would carry into effect; but his mind was not fertile and his inventive faculty was undeveloped.

Finally, Miller knocked the ashes out of his pipe, filled up, lighted, puffed, and then said: "Templeton, we're in a bad box; but it's a wise father who knows his own son, and I *hope* for the best. You know I have all along had my fears that Delaney would be in our way, so I investigated him. I believe, as firmly as I believe we live, that Delaney is Russell's son."

"The devil!" said Templeton.

"Yes, and all his angels," said Miller; "and if I only knew for certain, that he had lost his toe, I'd swear that he is Harry Russell. But, as you know, I have been busy in *our* matter, and this afternoon I followed up my Templeton suggestion, by giving Mr. Russell a report of your having gone to Nassau, of our Chief's writing to the consul there, and so on. He took it hard. He doesn't like you. His wife doesn't like you. And the daughter is worse than either of 'em. Still, he seems to be a square kind of a man, and if it turns out to his satisfaction, toe and all, that you are his son, in you go, and time must take care of the rest."

"Well, I don't see any very 'bad box' so far," said Templeton.

"Of course you don't, because I haven't shown it to you yet. The 'bad box' is made up of two important facts; their dislike of you, and their acquaintance with Robert Delaney."

"Whew! I see," said Templeton.

"And if to that," continued Miller, "they should in any particular distrust *me*, why up goes the sponge and the jig is over."

"Well, what's to be done?" asked Templeton.

"My idea is this. You go to New York, and stay there for about a week. On the arrival of a steamer from Nassau, have the papers announce the arrival of Lieut. William Templeton, U. S. N., at some first-class hotel. I'll show that to Mr. Russell, and at the same time I'll have a copy of a letter from the Consul to our Chief giving a good account of you, and telling all we want to know, *except the toe.* That we'll keep for a grand sensation. You can take the Pacific express to-morrow morning at ten, and from that on we must trust to luck, and stare fate in the face."

"All right, Miller," said Templeton; "you are a 'brick,' and ten to one we'll come out ahead in this matter yet. But how about Hardy? I understood from a paragraph in last night's paper that he was not doing well; had had a relapse or something."

"I don't know," replied Miller, "about that. I *do* know, however, that it's a mighty fortunate thing for us, that we have not had another smart fellow to bother. Why, he might have upset the whole affair, if he had been with me all the time. As it is, I never hear him mentioned without a shudder."

And so talking, these two worthies gradually neared the house, and were about entering when suddenly Miller stopped.

Catching his companion by the arm, he said: "Templeton, you know I like you, but, I don't value your whole carcase, soul included, as much as the least of the hairs of Mary's head. I have seen with some dread her regard for you; for I know you, root and branch. Still, if you are serious and the girl insists upon it I won't stand in your way. But—" and here Miller drew nearer to Templeton's ear, "if you are *not* serious, and aught of harm befalls my girl, expect no mercy from me. I'd shoot you like a dog."

Templeton endeavored to laugh and speak freely, but he failed.

He knew it, and Miller knew it.

The rest of the evening was passed pleasantly in the parlor, but Templeton retired first, instead of waiting as his custom was, until Miller and Martha had gone, that he might steal a farewell kiss from Mary.

CHAPTER XXXIII.

TWO PLAYING AT THE SAME GAME, ONE BADLY BEATEN.

JOHN HARDY'S arrival was an event in the hotel life of the Russell family.

Though not entirely strong, the young man was able to walk from the hospital door to the carriage, and when Mr. Russell offered assistance to help him up stairs at the hotel, it was declined as unnecessary.

A pleasant room adjoining Mr. Russell's *suite* had been engaged for Hardy under the name of Wilson, by which name he was to make the acquaintance of Miller.

Mrs. Russell and Maud had placed flowers on the table, and given to the room as home-like an air as was possible; but Hardy needed no other charm than that of the kindly grasp of the hand, and the undisguised delight in the countenance of every member of the little family, of whom for a brief period he was now to be part.

Hardy's mind was active, and worked rapidly. He had devoted much thought to the complication as reported by Mr. Russell at their last interview, and confessed himself embarrassed.

"If it can be *proven* that William Templeton was the identical Bob Delaney, what right," thought Hardy, "have I to throw discredit upon him?

"And if detective Miller has really done a good piece of work while I was laid up at the hospital, what right have I to appear as a marplot and upset all his operations?"

John Hardy was honest, as well as clever, but in this it would seem as if he were more honest than bright.

What if Templeton was Delaney?

Did that necessarily establish him as Harry Russell?

Old Miller thought further ahead than Hardy in this matter, although it will be remembered that, as yet, Hardy had never heard anything about an identification by means of the loss of a toe.

"Now, Hardy," began Mr. Russell, after they had talked over the hospital for the hundredth time, "Miller will be here this evening, and he expects me to give him my conclusion about Templeton. I will introduce you as my friend from Liverpool, Mr. George Wilson, button-maker, and as Miller goes on, you make up your mind. All you have to do is to indicate your ideas, and I'll follow them out to the letter. Mind you. I want to do the correct thing by every one. If I have wronged Templeton, I'll make amends—but I haven't."

Not long after this, Miller was announced. Mr. Russell introduced Hardy as an intimate friend from Liverpool, who being familiar with the whole story would make one of the council, on the occasion.

The two detectives looked at each other well.

Hardy was rather pleased with Miller's offhand way, and Miller saw swiftly a handsome-featured, well-built, honest-appearing youth, who looked straight out of his eyes, evidently afraid of nothing.

"Mr. Russell has been telling me of your success, Mr. Miller," said Hardy, "in tracing up little Bob Delaney, and of the most extraordinary coincidence that he should prove, probably, to be Mr. Templeton, a former fellow-passenger of his. Would you mind giving me, in detail, the plan you pursued? It must be very interesting, and I am sure it is most creditable to your ingenuity and skill as an officer."

Miller longed for his pipe.

It was difficult for him to think clearly without a pipe, and his lies were halting unless his head was enveloped in smoke.

But he was an experienced sinner.

A shrewd old fellow, whose game was honesty.

Looking from Hardy to the ladies, and then at Mr. Russell, Miller said: "Oh, I don't know about the in genuity, Mr. Wilson. It didn't require such an awful amount of headwork to find out that old Delaney had moved away. Then by tracking his old companions, and mine, I heard he was sent back to New York. Good luck helped me to the fact that the boy he had with him was shipped on an eastward-bound vessel, and the hospital record told the rest. It is a simple matter of fact, sir. We can't prove it by seeing the boy grow, but we can do what is just as good. We trace him by means of official documents to the date of his adoption, and from that moment the high school, college, and the navy stand as unimpeachable witnesses."

'Have you kept any memorandum of dates?" asked Hardy.

"Only in my head," replied Miller.

"Then this boy's name was —"

"Mr. Robert Delaney is below, sir, and asks if you are engaged," said a servant at the door.

"Mr. Robert Delaney?" said Hardy, springing to his feet; "surely not Templeton?"

Miller felt as if the floor was sinking from under his feet.

And Mr. Russell for the first time thought of the identity of the names of his young clerical friend, and the little Bob Delaney of his search.

For a moment there was danger of a scene, but Hardy recovered himself almost immediately, as did

Miller! Mr. Russell turning to his wife said: "I think you had better see Mr. Delaney in the parlor below, mother. Tell him we are very busy. He won't stay long, for he has a service, I am quite sure, at half-past seven."

"Excuse me, Mr. Russell," said Hardy; "why not ask Mr. Delaney here? If his name is Robert Delaney perhaps he can tell us something about Bob Delaney—and at all events I wish you would ask him up."

Miller said nothing, but he thought a great deal.

As yet he had no suspicion of Hardy's real business.

But he was fast growing to dislike him and to desire to avoid him.

Mr. Russell directed the waiter to show Mr. Delaney to their parlor, and presently the young clergyman appeared, bright-faced and cordial in his bearing.

He was glad to see the Russells and showed it.

He was surprised, however, to see Miller, and he showed that.

Mr. Russell it will be remembered had spoken of Hardy to Mr. Delaney and had promised himself much pleasure in bringing the young men together. But it was obviously impossible for him to present Hardy by his own name to Mr. Delaney while Miller was in the room; so he simply introduced the two, Hardy responding to the name of Wilson.

All they needed to complete the party was Tem

pleton—but he was on his way to New York as fast as steam and wheels could take him.

While Mr. Russell was for a few moments engaged in welcoming Mr. Delaney, and with the ladies formed a temporary group in the center of the room, Miller occupied himself in preparing for a retreat; and Hardy from his vantage ground made an estimate of his Chicago comrade.

Miller saw the dangerous ground on which he stood and determined to hold it only so long as it was wise to do so; resolving if any exposure should suddenly be made, to affect as great surprise as any, and to be as profoundly indignant as the best of them.

Hardy was troubled.

He felt distrust of Miller without knowing why, and believing Templeton to be a schemer and an adventurer, was resolved to trust him in nothing that was not proved to a mathematical certainty.

When they were all seated Mr. Russell said: "Do you know, Mr. Delaney, we were just talking about '"Bob Delaney' when the servant announced your name."

The clergyman looked astonished at what appeared a rather pronounced and unaccustomed liberty with his name, and smilingly replied: "Well, sir, I hope Bob Delaney was treated with all due respect. You mustn't forget that I am in my new house now, with at least a full cubit added to my stature."

This pleasantry did not meet with the expected recognition, and Mr. Delaney became so evidently confused, that Hardy, with his characteristic disregard of conventionalisms said: "Excuse me, Mr. Delaney, if at the risk of seeming over-curious, I ask you a question or two, bearing directly on the happiness of Mr. Russell."

Mr. Delaney bowed.

Miller sat as quiet as a cat.

"Your name is Robert Delaney. Has it always been so?"

"Certainly," replied the clergyman.

"Are you a native of Chicago?"

"That I cannot answer, but I have lived here since I was a boy. My history is well known to my fellow-citizens."

"Is there any uncertainty or mystery about your birth or early childhood?"

"None, that I am aware of."

"Is your father living?"

"No. He died here many years since. He was a builder and fell —"

"A *what?*" shouted Hardy; "a *builder?*" "Mr. Russell, do you hear that? A builder? And his name, what was that?"

"James Delaney," answered the clergyman, half bewildered and wholly surprised.

"Thank God! thank God!" said Hardy. "Why,

Mr. Miller, your man Templeton is a liar, and a fraud and a scoundrel, sir. I know it. I can prove it. I have *felt* it in my bones from the first. Now I know it."

"And you," said Miller, utterly disconcerted; "for Heaven's sake who, and what are *you?*"

"I," rejoined Hardy; "I am John Hardy of the New York office, at your service, Mr. Miller, and I only hope I shall find in you as square a man as I try to be."

Words fail in the attempt to picture the overwhelming gratification of Mr. Russell, the sympathizing and admiring glances of Mrs. Russell and Maud, the helpless curiosity of Mr. Delaney, and the consternation of Miller.

"I hope," stammered out Miller, "you don't for a moment imagine that *I*"—

"Oh, I don't imagine anything," interrupted Hardy; "imagination is very well in its way, but what we want is *facts*. I know this fellow Templeton, root and branch. He tried to bribe me in New York, and I expected to cross his trail here. I must say he played a pretty bold game, and if he deceived you, he is a clever fellow indeed. But how is it that you never heard of Mr. Delaney?"

"Well, that is good," said Mr. Delaney, who was still in the dark. "Mr. Miller has known me, and of me, these twenty years, and his home is one of my resorts. And by the way, Mr. Miller, this coincidence of names is strange, is it not? I was telling the ladies the other evening, that your pretty Mary is betrothed to a gentleman by the name of Russell, Harry Russell is it not? And here I am"—

Hardy could keep quiet no longer. Impetuously he broke in on the unfinished sentence with "Mr. Miller, you are an older man than I, and possibly a better officer, but my position in this matter ranks yours. You may consider yourself relieved until I have seen your Chief. I will call on him to-morrow, and I promise you then a full investigation of this most extraordinary case. If the result is satisfactory, I will apologize to you for my suspicion; as it is now, I cannot advise Mr. Russell to treat you with further confidence."

Miller was a man of the world, hardened, callous, and indifferent to opinion, but the fiery indignation of the young officer, cut him to the quick.

But he showed no feeling whatever. Taking his hat, he said: "I will see you, Mr. Wilson, or Hardy, or whatever your name may be, at the office to-morrow; and if you think you've seen and heard the last of 'One-eyed Charley,' you mistake your man."

As Miller went out Hardy stepped up to him and quietly said: "Take my advice, and make a clean breast of it. I know Templeton, and I know you. Good-night."

After Miller's departure, explanations were made, and Mr. Delaney repeated the story of his boyhood, his father's habits and terrible death, and his general life as known to the reader.

The early hours of the following day, found the three men still in consultation, and when they separated it was understood :

That Mr. Delaney was little "Bob" grown up ;

That he was undeniably the son of James Delaney, the builder ;

That therefore little Bob and Harry Russell, were not identical ;

That Mr. Delaney's love for Martha Miller should screen the lady's father from exposure and disgrace, on condition that he laid bare Templeton's programme ; for although there was no proof as yet, that Miller had ever seen Templeton, it *was* evident that the two were working together to establish the Lieutenant as little Bob, and doubtless to continue the deception down to the very door of the Russell home.

Mr. Delaney left Mr. Russell and Hardy together, the one down-hearted because his time was wasted, and nothing gained ; the latter weary and fatigued, but thankful that he had been the means of breaking up what he believed to be an atrocious conspiracy ; and happy too in the belief that he was not indifferent to Maud, or her parents.

It would be difficult to say, what Mr. Russell dreamed of that night.

But Hardy dreamed of fairy land, with Maud as queen.

CHAPTER XXXIV.

A SOFT ANSWER TURNS AWAY WRATH.

EARLY on the following morning, Monday, Maud, who was a perfect kitten with her mother, drew a small footstool near Mrs. Russell's chair in their parlor, and resting her folded hands upon that good lady's knee, looked up in her face, and said: "Mamma, papa is very angry with Miller, isn't he?"

"Yes, dear, I think he is; why not?"

"And is he angry at Templeton, too?"

"That depends. Mr Hardy intimates that he has reason to believe Templeton to be, not only an unprincipled person, but a plotter against your father of the meanest description. After retiring last night father was very nervous. He could not sleep, and seeing how excited he was, I canvassed the whole affair with him. He trusts, as I do, everything to Hardy, and will undoubtedly be guided entirely by him. It now looks as if we should all go back to New York immediately. This time is all lost, and instead of gaining any good, we seem to have had simply annoyance and distress."

"You surely do not regret meeting Mr. Delaney," said Maud, "and one would think Hardy was one of us, I am sure. I declare he is like an own brother to me,—only more respectful. But do you think Mr. Hardy will do anything dreadful to Templeton?"

"You silly girl," replied Mrs. Russell; "you surely cannot have a particle of feeling for a man, who—"

Maud stood straight up.

"Yes, mamma, I *have* a feeling. I have just *this* feeling, that I should hate above all things to have William Templeton imagine for one single moment that anything he might do, could cause my father one second's annoyance. I would have him treated with absolute contempt."

Mrs. Russell looked long and lovingly, at her excited daughter, and then taking her hand, said: "My darling, I think we can safely leave all this dreadful business to your father and his adviser; but I promise you, dear, that before any harsh proceedings are inaugurated, you shall know of them, and nothing shall be done which can in the remotest degree affect you or put it in Templeton's power to think his treatment of you, is the slightest motive in his disgrace."

Mr. Russell and John Hardy had been for some time in the reading-room, where Hardy had gone for the purpose of communicating with his headquarters in New York.

As they entered, Mr. Russell noticed Maud's flushed face, and with some anxiety, asked if she were not feeling well.

The young girl kissed away her father's fear, and extending her hand to Hardy, said: "Oh, Mr. Hardy, what an angel you are! A perfect angel of deliverance. How stupid we all are. Papa is just as bad as the rest of us. Why, do you know we met Mr. Delaney at a party, and he talked, and walked with me a long time. We have been to his church, and his card with that very name printed on it, has been in my hands half a dozen times at least. And yet till you fired it out at us, like a cannon ball, not one of us even *dreamed* that there was the very man we wanted."

"And now we find he is the very man we don't want," laughed Hardy.

"But a very fine fellow, for all that," said Mr. Russell.

"Yes, indeed he is," said Maud; "and a lovely preacher. You ought to hear him. He never writes a sermon. All he has is on a little bit of paper. But he knows what to say, and how to say it."

"I was a little staggered, wasn't you, Mr. Russell," asked Hardy, "when he told us he was engaged to one of old Miller's daughters, and thought he should be married in a short time?"

"Yes, I was," replied Mr. Russell; "and it bothers me now."

"Why, father?" said his wife.

"Why, if Miller has been playing us false—as he has—he deserves to be broken, and punished. I trusted him. I turned myself inside out before him. I made him welcome. I paid him well, and if he cheated me—and he has—he has been not only wicked, but mean. Of course he should be exposed. Exposure means disgrace and ruin."

"Well," said Hardy.

"Well, his daughters are good girls, I am told. You know what Delaney says of them. And you know what we all think of Delaney. Whatever hurts Miller, hurts his children. And whatever hurts them hurts Delaney. And what hurts Delaney, hurts me."

"Oh father, dear, dear father. Who wouldn't be fond of such a father," said Maud, and the impulsive girl threw her arms about him, and kissed him again and again.

Hardy looked on with interest. Everything about Maud Russell charmed him. The affection she manifested for her parents was simple and genuine. Her kindliness was always apparent. Her thoughtfulness of others' comfort and happiness and ease never slept.

Happy to be of service to her, he said: "I think, Miss Russell, it will be easy to manage Miller, so that while his daughters shall be spared all mortification, he can be useful to your father. I gave him an intimation last night, on which I think he will act. If he thought fighting would bring him and his man Templeton safely through he would fight; but he must see, and if he doesn't he will before we get through with him, that he has lost the game, and granting that, he will be very apt to make terms as best as he can. I propose to say to him that if he will disclose the entire scheme, of which he is part, for his daughters' sake, Mr. Russell will forgive his offense."

"But how about Templeton?" asked Mrs. Russell.

"Well, Templeton has no daughter that I know of, and he's not only bad, but a sneak," said Hardy.

"But what is gained by following these wretches?" said Maud.

"Why, daughter," said Mr. Russell, "are we still tender on the Lieutenant; mustn't we punish anybody?"

Mrs. Russell caught her husband's eye, and with a glance, delivered a protest more eloquent than words could express, and like a model man he changed his tactics at once.

"Hardy," said he, "we will send for Miller and compromise on your terms. To-night we will go to Parson Delaney's house-warming, and see his pretty bride, that is to be, and to-morrow start for New York. 'Little Bob' we have found. 'Little Harry' is still to *be* found. We drop old Miller, push Templeton from our thoughts, and make one final effort for my boy. If we find him you shall go home with us, to see the royal welcome he will have. And if we fail, why then you *must* go home with us, to rest yourself a while and to comfort me."

Mrs. Russell and Maud went out to make some purchases, their donations to the young pastor; Hardy wrote and sent a note to Miller, requesting his presence at the hotel; and M. Russell busied himself with his correspondence.

As Hardy, having dispatched his message, turned to go to his own room to rest, Mr. Russell rose, and taking him by the hand said: "Hardy, my boy, don't think I am unmindful of your solicitude and helpfulness. I am not a talker. I feel your kindness, and am grateful for it. Be assured, young man, I shall not forget it."

CHAPTER XXXV.

THE SURPRISERS SURPRISED.

MONDAY evening was memorable in the life of the Rev. Robert Delaney.

His parishioners had arranged a "surprise donation party" for him, but, as is always the case, the fact leaked out, and being something of a wag, the young parson thought he would meet his people on their own ground, and beat them at their own game.

The only invitations Mr. Delaney issued were to the Russell family, and John Hardy, a clerical friend and Charles Miller, the detective.

Each of these he asked, begging them on no account to be later than nine o'clock, and if possible to reach the house half an hour earlier.

At eight o'clock the good folks began to arrive, bearing gifts of every sort and name, from the ponderous barrel of flour in an express wagon, to the delicate Parian *vase* in the fair hands of the giver. Eatables sufficient to "keep" a moderate-sized family an entire season were left at the basement door. Articles of chamber utility and of parlor adornment were handed in in marvellous abundance, while the study and the bookcase were liberally remembered.

Mr. Russell and his party arrived early, and were especially pleased at the unmistakable earnestness and cordiality of the greetings between pastor and people. "I tell you, mother," said Mr. Russell, "that's the kind of a minister for me. He knows every one of these people, and they love him like a brother. No question about it, that young man will do a power of good here. I wonder if he wouldn't like to spend a few years with us."

The rooms were full, and Hardy was looking, with Maud, at a beautiful edition of De Quincey, when Mr. Delaney approached them, and said: "Mr. Hardy, I understand you had a long and satisfactory talk with Mr. Miller this afternoon."

"Yes, sir," replied Hardy; "and the old rascal owned up like a brick. Mind you, I don't mean anything disrespectful to you in what I say about Miller. Miller isn't his daughter by a long way. Yes, Miller gave me some very important assistance, and I must say I like the way he acted about Templeton. He owned up that he and Templeton put up this Bob Delaney job, and said if it hadn't been for my noticing the similarity of the name with yours, he would have convinced not only Mr. Russell, but the ladies and perhaps myself, that Templeton really was little Bob. Beyond that confession he insisted it was not fair to expect him to go. I am convinced that in some way he expected to connect little Bob with the lost Harry; but how I could not divine. For the sake of Martna Miller, indeed I may say for your sake, sir, Miller is as free to-day as you are. We will do him no harm. And not only that, but I volunteered the promise that if he would write such a letter to Templeton as would scare the scoundrel from New York, I would never mention to the chief of police here our dissatisfaction or Miller's infidelity."

"I am very thankful to you, I am sure," said Mr. Delaney. "I have prepared a little surprise for Miller and for all my guests to-night, which I hope will not be displeasing to you, to both of you, and if you will kindly join Mr. and Mrs. Russell in the front parlor, you will have a better opportunity of understanding me."

Of course they went, Maud saying, as they passed through the crowd of friends: "I think Mr. Delaney is a very nice person, don't you? I am almost sorry he is not our Harry, after all."

Mrs. Russell had asked Mr. Delaney to present her to Martha Miller, but he replied that neither she nor her sister had arrived. Later in the evening Mrs. Russell reminded her host of her request, and he made the same reply.

When Hardy and Maud joined Mr. and Mrs. Russell, the latter said to Hardy : " Have you seen either of Miller's daughters, Mr. Hardy? I want very much to meet them, and especially Miss Martha. She is Mr. Delaney's betrothed, you know, and he seems very proud of her."

" Well, yes, I should say I do know it," said Hardy, " considering it has altered all my plans, saved Miller, and kept Templeton out of jail. I am free to confess I would like to see what kind of a daughter such a father can have."

Mr. Russell kept suspiciously quiet. He had had a long conversation with Mr. Delaney quite early in the evening, and had been very thoughtful ever since ; so much so that both Maud and her mother rallied him on his absentmindedness.

Precisely at nine o'clock the door opening into the hall near the front door swung on its hinges, and four beautiful girls, of whom Mary Miller was one, entered, separating two by two, as they semi-circled at the end of the room, while Martha Miller, leaning on the arm of Robert Delaney took her place in the centre.

So complete was the surprise of everybody in the room, that no one noticed the entrance of the brother minister, nor of old Miller, who quietly took a position near the door.

Mr. Russell enjoyed the scene immensely. To

him alone the secret had been confided, and only to him on Miller's account.

Well, a bride is a bride, even if she weds a clergyman.

And a wedding is a wedding, be it in a garret or castle.

It was soon over.

But the night was far spent ere the congratulations were over, and the house was emptied of all but the bride and groom, their sister Mary, and old Miller.

The old man was rather out of his element, but as Mary and he rose to bid Delaney and his wife good-night, Miller swung his hat in his hand, and said: "Robert, from this hour you shall have no cause for uneasiness about me or mine. I shall resign my position to-morrow. Mary tells me she *must* have a change of scene. So must I. These girls are all I cared for in life. To them I now add you. God bless you. In a little while, a few days at most, Mary and I go west for a tramp. I don't know but we'll take in California and the Sandwich Islands—anywhere and anything to please her and change myself. So don't worry, Martha; you've got a good husband. Good-night, and God bless you."

The girls hung about their father's neck and kissed him, while Robert Delaney grasped his hand, and bade him always be sure of a hearty welcome in the home of his son and daughter.

CHAPTER XXXVI.

WALKING DOWN BROADWAY.

THE Russells had returned to New York some two weeks, when John Hardy, who had left them at Chicago, for a few days' visit in Milwaukee, rejoined them.

"Well, Hardy," said Mr. Russell, after a few moments' natural inquiry, "what of the Millers, and how is my friend Robert?"

"I called on Mr. Delaney the day I left," replied Hardy, "and told him what you said about his going over to your place for a month, and he promised to lay the matter before his people. If they consent, he will go; his church is out of debt, and he received your generous offer to pay all expenses in precisely the spirit you made it. He is a splendid fellow I think, and that wife of his is just as nice as she can be."

"And how about Mary Miller," said Mrs. Russell.

"Well, she's in trouble," said Hardy. "I don't understand exactly what it is. I only know that she is now living with the Delaneys, and old Miller is fairly wild about something, of which he won't speak. He wrote to Templeton the day after the wedding, gave him all the points, and advised him to leave the country until your departure rendered it safe to return. Miller had a terrible time with Mary, and Delaney tells me the poor girl was frantic with grief, when her father told her of her lover's perfidy. I imagine he only told her part of it at that time. Templeton has gone to South America, but before he went, he wrote Mary a pretty rough kind of a letter: not ugly, as men look at such things, but killing to a woman. She drooped and faded, and was very sick, and while she was hanging between life and death, she told Mrs. Delaney something or other that stirred old Miller up fearfully, and when I got back to Chicago, the old man came to me with fire in his eye and said he would come on with me, as he had business with Templeton. I was rather surprised at that and said, 'Why, he's gone to South America;' to which he replied, 'He *said* he was going, but I would not believe the scoundrel under oath. It's lucky for him if he has gone.' So I infer that something pretty bad has happened."

"Oh, I am *so* sorry," said Maud.

"Yes, indeed," echoed her mother.

"Well, go on, go on," said Mr. Russell; "where is Miller now?"

"I sent him to French's Hotel, down by the City Hall," said Hardy. "He wanted to be at some central point, and handy to the wharves. I don't know what to do with him. I don't like him, but it doesn't seem exactly fair to snub him. And then if I could do anything for his daughter, I should be very glad."

"Yes, and we, too," said Mrs. Russell. "I suppose you wouldn't care to see him, would you, father?"

"No. That is, unless Hardy thought I could be of service to the girl. I can't say I regard a man who conspired against my heart and property, with any special liking. Hardy, you do what's best, and I'll back you. Now, my boy, I have written to my people, that I shall leave the States six weeks fron to-day. Until then, we must strain every nerve for the accomplishment of our purpose. And then—well, if then there is no clue and no hope, I shall at all events be relieved of a burden I have carried these long, long years. I have done my duty. Would that I had succeeded. And I have a little project in my head about you, of which we will speak another time. By the way, Hardy, don't you think it would be well for me to call on the Mayor, and thank him for his courtsey and letters? I haven't seen him since the first week of my arrival."

"Just as you please about that," said Hardy; 'he's a nice old gentleman, very kind-hearted and one of the regular old school."

"I suppose it will be necessary to send word sev eral days in advance."

"Oh, no," said Hardy; "we'll jump on a car any day and go right in. His office hours are supposed to be from ten to three. There's no trouble about seeing him yourself."

"Why can't we go somewhere this evening, papa," asked Maud.

"Where do you want to go, dear?"

"Oh, anywhere. What is going on, Mr. Hardy?"

Hardy looked at the paper, and after scanning its amusement columns, said: "I see they are playing 'Led Astray' at the Union Square Theatre, right a the foot of the square here. How would you like that?"

"Well, I'm sure we've been led astray," said Mrs. Russell, "suppose we go and see others in the same predicament."

"Will you get seats, Hardy?" said Mr. Russell.

"Tickets for four, Mr. Hardy," said Maud.

Hardy looked quickly at Mr. Russell, who simply smiled and said: "You did not suppose he would get a dozen, did you, dear?"

"Why, no; but you know what I mean, papa," she answered.

Mr. Russell thought he did know, but he held his own counsel and said nothing.

Arranging to join the party at dinner, Hardy, whc

had become one of the family in the estimation of all, bade them good-morning, and intimating to Mr. Russell to join him, left the room.

Mr. Russell followed, and together they walked down to the theatre. There were no seats, and they were compelled to take a box or nothing.

"Of all places in these New York theatres," said Mr. Russell, "the boxes are most uncomfortable. Two people can see about two-thirds of the stage; and the others are lucky, if they see a quarter."

"Well; I suppose people who sit in boxes, as a rule, care more for the audience than the actors," suggested Hardy.

"What an idea," said Mr. Russell; "what do you suppose I care about the audience?"

"The ladies might, if you didn't."

"Nonsense. If I thought my wife or Maud went to the theatre to look at the people, I'd——"

"You'd let them do just what they wanted," laughed Hardy.

"Yes, I dare say I would," said Mr. Russell. "Where are you going now?"

"I was going down to the Central Office," said Hardy; "but if you would like to call on the Mayor now, I'll take you there."

"All right," said Mr. Russell; "but why not go down Broadway instead of by the cars. I would very much like to walk down part way at least."

Taking the west side of New York's greatest highway, the two friends, arm in arm, proceeded down, meeting scores of thousands of busy, bustling people, rich and poor, wise and foolish, like the rest of the world.

Hardy knew all the notables, and as they passed pointed them out to his companion.

"Here comes one of our Congressmen," said he, "he's a gambler now, and used to be a prize-fighter, but he's one of our political powers to-day."

"You surely do not mean that a man can be in Congress and be a gambler at the same time," said Mr. Russell.

"Why, certainly," replied Hardy; "why not? You see our city politics are curiously managed. We have two great parties, the Republican and the Democratic. All the foreigners are 'taken' with the name of the latter, and make haste to join it. Some of them are so delighted, that they not only join the party, but vote at the polls before they've been twelve months in the country."

"Bless my soul," said Mr. Russell. "But they rarely hold office I imagine, do they?"

"Your imagination does you discredit," said Hardy; "they hold it all the time. Look at the policemen we meet between this and the City Hall. Here come three now. What are they?"

"Evidently Irishmen," said Mr. Russell.

"Precisely. All Irish. We have hosts of Irishmen on the force."

"Do they make good officers?"

"That depends. During the war riots, the police acted nobly. It was feared that their sympathies for the poor devils who were dragged off to the war, would affect them in the performance of their duty. But not at all. They obeyed orders like soldiers. The city was saved by their heroism."

"But your aldermen and so on, of course, as a rule, they are natives."

"Not at all. As a rule they are adopted citizens. Aldermen as a general thing are not remarkable for wit or honesty. Their stupidity is proverbial. Our sheriff is an Irishman. The county clerk is a German. Three of the coroners are German, and in all our local boards—such as school trustees, excise commissioners, ward officers and so on—the foreign element is largely represented."

"How do you account for that?" said Mr. Russell. "It seems very strange to me."

"Oh, easily," answered Hardy; "the party in power has all the 'patronage,' as it is called. Patronage here means public employment. The police, the fire department, the parks, the public works, the court officers, all are cursed by the same complaint. The party in power wants all the places to pay for services rendered at the polls. Thousands of laborers are paid two dollars a day on the boulevards for instance, and every man of them has his work because some politician asked it. Why, even the policemen don't know from day to day how long they are secure in their places."

"But doesn't the Mayor attend to—"

"The Mayor!" said Hardy; "the Mayor has just about as much to do with it as you have. He can't make nor break a single employé of the entire city government; not one of them, outside his individual office, is at his disposal."

"But surely he controls the finances, and the man who does that is in the seat of power?"

"Just so. *If* he controlled the finances. But he controls nothing. Our financial chief is well called the comptroller. When he is notified that bills are to be paid or money expended, he makes out a warrant and signs it. The Mayor countersigns it as a matter of form. He knows nothing about it. If he refuses to sign it, the courts will compel him. I tell you the Mayor is a perfect cipher. All he can do is to receive people, review processions, respond to toasts, and be a respectable dummy figure-head. Do you see that man, the tall one, on the corner? That's Lester Wallack."

"Who is he?"

"Well, he owns the theatre I showed you on the corner of 13th street. He is considered our best

American comedian, and is a great favorite in society, as well as on the stage."

"He looks a manly fellow," said Mr. Russell; "is he a New Yorker?"

"Oh, no. He's an Englishman, son of the great Wallack, and a very fine man."

"What a solid, respectable-looking edifice that is! What is it?" asked Mr. Russell.

"That's Stewart's retail store. He has another about as large further down town."

"Rich man, I suppose?"

"Well I should say so. He is reported as having about $75,000,000."

"Bless my soul. Did he make or inherit it?"

"Made every dollar of it."

"Born here?"

"No. He's Irish, or Scotch-Irish I believe."

"It seems to me everything and everybody has a touch of Irish or English in this town, Hardy."

"It does look so, I declare. Let's see; they are playing either French, English or Irish pieces at all the theatres. Nearly all our leading actors are foreign. A majority of our politicians came from County Cork, and nearly every beggar one meets has a brogue on his tongue, or has left his h's at 'ome.'

"Those are fine photographs, Hardy. Let me take the number of this place. Maud was saying last night she must have some pictures taken. Suppose we step in a moment."

They looked at the collection in which Hardy pointed out Edwin Booth, President Grant, Governor Dix, Mayor Havemeyer, Mrs. Scott Siddons, Miss Rose Eytinge, Rev. H. W. Beecher, Miss Charlotte Cushman, P. T. Barnum, General Sherman, James Fisk, Jr., and other well known people, after which Mr. Russel engaged an hour for Mrs. Russell and daughter the following day.

As they regained the street Hardy noticed the time and said he feared it would be too late to find the Mayor at his office.

Mr. Russell was about replying when his eye caught the figure of One-eyed Charley Miller.

Miller was walking rapidly on the opposite side of the street.

His hat was pulled well down over his forehead, but his figure and gait were unmistakable.

Hardy, without a word to Mr. Russell, ran after Miller, and surprised him before he had time to think or speak.

" Hallo, old man, where are you going in such a hurry?" said Hardy.

Miller stopped short.

His hair was disordered, his eye was bloodshot, his face unshaven, his linen soiled, his clothing untidy.

He was drunk.

"Hardy," said he; "damn you, Hardy, old fel; I like you. Say, Hardy, I want to get my flippers on that Templeton. Hardy, I'm drunk; and when I'm drunk I know it. I don't stagger outside, and I don't stagger inside. Where's Russell, Hardy? I like Russell. Let's get a drink."

Mr. Russell crossed the street and was approaching the two, but Hardy motioned him away and he retired to a doorway, where he could see what occurred.

Hardy was very anxious to get from Miller the whole of Templeton's plan, and this he believed to be a good time to do so. He hailed a *coupé* and pulling Miller in, told the man to drive to police headquarters, and jumped in himself. And so, for a second time, Mr. Russell was unceremoniously left to find his way home alone.

CHAPTER XXXVII.

JOHN AND MAUD.

AT the dinner table, Mr. Russell complained of headache, and told his wife he would have to be excused from going with her to the theatre, and that she and Maud must depend on Hardy for an escort.

While they were discussing the matter, Hardy came in, and Mrs. Russell said: "Mr. Hardy, we old folks will stay at home together to-night. You take Maud to the theatre; she is very anxious to go, and I am very glad I have so trusty a friend to send her with."

"I shall be very glad to escort Miss Maud, I am sure," said Hardy, "but I think you make a mistake in not going."

"Oh, I have a bad headache, Hardy," said Mr. Russell, "and I'm not going. So you just take good care of Maud, and be sure to let me see you early in the morning. Where did you leave your friend?"

"Oh, he's all right," replied Hardy; "I left him fast asleep at headquarters in the matron's apartments.

He will be brought to my room in the morning; and, by the way, suppose you look in about noon. You know the way, don't you?"

"All right, I will," said Mr. Russell, as they rose from the table, and Maud retired to dress.

Presently returning, the pride and pet of the happy pair, Maud kissed her father and mother good-by, and gay as a lark, started off with the happiest and proudest of them all—John Hardy, her lover yet un announced.

The beautiful theatre was crowded, every seat being taken, and the audience peculiarly bright and gay In the orchestra stalls sat many people of repute, known personally or by sight to Hardy, and the time passed quickly as they waited for the rising of the curtain.

The play was full of suggestive points, all of which Hardy felt; some of which made Maud wonder.

At the close of the second act, Maud was in ecstasies. She had not often attended theatrical representations, and the excitement told upon her. She was bewilderingly beautiful, and many a glass was turned full upon her flushed and innocent face, as unconscious of the attention she looked out upon the people.

"Your father asked me to engage rooms on the steamer to-day," said Hardy.

"I know it," said Maud; "I am very sorry. A

month will give us very little time here. I am just beginning to know New York, and I wanted to see Niagara before we went home. You don't know how pleasant it is, to have you with us, Mr. Hardy. Mamma said to-day, she should miss you awfully when we part."

"And you?"

"Oh, you know I shall. I am sure you have been better to me than any brother. From the dreadful hour when you saved me from injury, if not from death, you have been even more than a brother *could* be."

"I wish I might. That is, I wish it were possible for me to be where I might always be of service to you, Miss Maud. The kindness and sympathy shown me by your father touch me very nearly, I assure you, and when he goes, I shall feel as if the world were dark indeed."

"But papa says you are going over with us," said Maud. "He says you need rest, and he's going to get it for you. You won't spoil all our plans, will you? Say you won't, please."

Hardy said nothing. He loved the girl devotedly, but he loved her honorably. He would have given ten years of his life to feel that he had the right to woo her, but he feared it would not be fair towards the parents who trusted him.

"Well, I declare, Mr. Hardy," said Maud, "you are as sober as a judge. Why don't you answer me?"

"Really, I cannot. I don't know that I can get leave of absence, and besides, I—"

"You what? I believe my soul there's something romantic in all this. It isn't pretty Mary Miller, is it?"

And Maud laughed merrily as she asked the question.

"Come, come, Mr. Hardy, I'll tell papa if you don't entertain me. Is there a lady in the case?"

"Yes, a dear sweet lady, the dearest, and sweetest in the world."

"And won't she let you go to Europe?"

Hardy looked at her.

He loved her, and he hoped she knew it, although he had never said it.

He was sitting at her side, but back so that he neither saw the audience, nor could be seen by it.

Maud turned toward Hardy and he, impulsive in spite of his caution, took her hand firmly in his and with an earnestness too marked to be trifled with said: "Maud, *you* are that lady. For you I have perilled life, but it was as nothing. I have loved you since we met. I hated and pursued that scoundrel because he was playing with your love. I began to take a deep interest in serving your father, because I loved you, though in the service I grew to love him. To please you is my ambition, to win you would be a reward of which at least I have a right to think, if not to hope for. You are dearer to me than life. Your love I would prize above all earthly blessings. Am I rash in telling you this? Do I offend? I would not have spoken had I counselled of my pride, but asking Love, I dared to speak. May I have hope?"

Maud's color came and died away. She knew that Hardy's manliness was as honest and trustworthy as that of her father.

She respected, esteemed, admired him, but did she love him?

She allowed her hand to remain in his for a moment.

Then smiling sweetly she withdrew it, and said: "Thank you, Mr. Hardy. I thank you. You have neither annoyed nor offended me. I will tell you more when we leave this place."

"But may I hope?"

"Yes, hope."

"I will speak to your father to-morrow. I will tell him of my love for you. I will beg him to lay aside his prejudice. I will—"

"Will you go home with us?"

"Yes, to the end of the earth."

The play proceeded on the stage and when the curtain fell on the final scene, so near as we can judge, the dramatic unities both in front and behind the footlights were in a remarkable state of harmony.

Maud and Hardy walked slowly back to the hotel —he an accepted lover, she a hopeful, happy girl.

CHAPTER XXXVIII.

AT LAST. AT LAST.

HE next morning Hardy was up bright and early, at peace with himself and all the world.

He was in love with Maud, and she with him.

What more could man desire?

What more?

Oh, *that* it was that made him ponder the past, consider the present and forecast the future.

In the past he saw the son of a scavenger.

In the present he beheld a detective police officer.

And in the future—what?

Would Mr. Russell, rich, influential, stern and proud, give the hand of his daughter to a man whose hundreds of dollars numbered less than his own scores of thousands?

And Mrs. Russell, kind and indulgent as she always was, would it be possible to induce her to so great a sacrifice?

These and kindred questions sobered his elated

heart and toned down his buoyant spirit, until apprehension took the place of peace, and doubt reigned supreme in the young man's mind.

He had no fear as to Maud.

Before he parted from her at the hotel she had given him ample assurance of her love, and together they had planned that the best way to approach Mr. Russell was through his wife.

That Maud undertook to do.

The dear girl knew that her mother's heart was bound up in her happiness, and that once a party to her daughter's project, nothing could turn or swerve her from her purpose.

Hardy lived in lodgings and took his meals at an adjacent restaurant. On this occasion he breakfasted unusually early, so that when old Miller was brought to his rooms he would be sure to be at home.

Having read the papers, Hardy naturally thought about Maud.

And that led him to think of his mother and of a picture he had of her, which he had promised to show to Maud.

He took the fading daguerreotype from its place on the mantel, and looked long and lovingly at the seamed and wrinkled face disclosed. It was not a handsome face, but it was his mother's. How well he remembered her kind care and thoughtful ways. She was always very fond of him, and shared her husband's pride in all his progress at school. And when he grew tall and manly, and began to bring home the fruits of his industry, her old eyes often filled with tears of gratitude, and her trembling lips uttered many prayers of thanks that the boy of her love was not like the rude and reckless companions of his age.

Her old-fashioned, nail-studded, hair-covered trunk stood in one corner of Hardy's room.

Years ago he had opened it once and saw bundles and books, and papers and letters, none of which he looked at.

Miller had not yet arrived, and the thought occurred to Hardy that this was a good time for him to empty the trunk, examine its contents, throw away the useless matter, and rearrange the rest.

Suiting the action to the thought, he hauled the trunk from its corner, opened it, and turned its contents on the bed.

As he did so, a knock was heard at the door.

"Come in," said Hardy.

"All right," said a voice, and in walked "One-eyed Miller."

"They were going to send a 'cop' round with me," said he; "but when they told me the way, I found it myself; and here I am, as straight as a ruler, but I want a pipe."

"I am glad to see you, Miller," said Hardy; "you

were seedy enough yesterday. Why, how nice you look. Been to a barber's?"

"Yes," said Miller, as he puffed fast and strong. "Yes, I wanted to see the old man and make it all right. I don't worry much about my conscience, you know, but Mary and Martha have been at me about it, till it seemed as if there was a little hell inside of me. I can't find that infernal scoundrel of a Templeton, with his black eye and curly hair. I'd Templeton him so quick, he wouldn't know which end he stood on if I had a chance at him. What are you doing with that kit of papers? Heavens, what a lot of letters! I hate letters. That is, all but the girls' letters. Every letter my girls ever wrote to me, I've got, and some of them are very good, I tell you."

If Miller had blustered, Hardy would have met him.

If he had commenced to lie, Hardy would have humored him.

As it was, Miller was fast making a conquest. Hardy knew enough of Miller's daughters to convince him that, prior to Templeton's advent, their home was happy and they contented. And he now knew that in some way Templeton had not only endeavored to deceive and practice fraud on Mr. Russell, but had done, through Mary, a great wrong to old Miller himself.

Sitting on the edge of the bed, while Miller took a

chair, Hardy said: "Miller, if I had gone into this job for money, and had been successful, I would have made a fortune. As it is, if my own interest was all I thought of, I might haul in a very big pile. You know enough of men in general, and of Mr. Russell especially, to see that. And you have done enough business with me to know that I am a man who deals on the square, and tells the truth. I not only haven't made a dollar out of this, but I don't intend to. Mr. Russell was not sanguine at the first, and to do him justice, he always agreed with me that the Bob Delaney boy was much more likely to be Bob Delaney than Harry Russell. Still, the search has done the old man a benefit; it has relieved his mind. He has done all he could, and that's all any man can be asked to do. *I* had a chance to go in with Templeton; the same you had. I didn't bluff him at first, I let him go on, and if I hadn't found him at the Tombs, trying to honeyfugle mother Foster, I think I should have given him just rope enough to hang himself with. Then he tried it on you, and I make no bones of telling you, you played a deucedly dirty trick on one of the best men living. And besides—but, never mind, we won't go into that."

"No," said Miller. "You're right; it was a mean game, but let bygones be bygones, I'm willing."

Hardy laughed, and went on:

"Of course you are. Now, you have done the

square thing by us because you had to, and you must admit that you've only done it as far as you were forced to; don't you think you would do a better thing if you were to tell me the whole plot from end to end? It won't harm you; it may lead to the punishment of Templeton."

As Hardy finished the sentence, he rose from the bed on which he was sitting, intending to lower a curtain, so as to shut out the sun, which shone directly in his face. As he did so, his foot tripped on the top of the trunk as it lay on the floor, and to save himself he caught quickly at the coverlid of the bed. This disarranged the bundles and papers, some of which were thrown upon the floor.

Miller assisted Hardy in picking them up, and as he did so, said: "Hallo, Hardy, what's this? Here's a bundle all tied up and sealed up as if it was a mummy. I declare, I haven't seen so much sealing wax since I was a boy. Seems to me you're not over careful of your jewelry."

Miller pitched the package to Hardy, who was about to place it with the rest, when he saw in his mother's cramped and awkward hand, his own name, written on the paper.

The bundle was soft, and apparently contained clothing.

Miller eyed him curiously.

"Why don't you open it?" said he.

Hardy said nothing, but felt of the package from end to end.

Then taking his knife from his pocket, he cut the strings.

Inside the paper was a roll of clothing, and a letter addressed

"JOHN HARDY,

"New York.

"If dead, destroy this."

Hardy was astounded.

For years that trunk had been under his very eye.

He had opened it but twice since it came in his possession.

Its contents he had never looked at nor cared for, although he had now and then thought he would at some time clean out the rubbish, and preserve whatever was worth keeping.

Yet in that trunk was a letter from the dearest mother man ever had.

He loved her living, and he loved her dead.

She had been so much to him that he never thought of her without a smile or a tear; and yet for years within reach of his hand had been this letter.

"Why, Miller," said he, "this is mother's. This letter's from mother. What can it be? Why have I never seen it before? I want to read it, yet I do not. Here, you read it. No, give it to me. What an idea! Bless her heart! That's her picture, Miller.

Bless her heart! She was just the best mother boy or man ever had. I'll read the letter."

Forgetting Miller and all else besides, Hardy opened the carefully sealed envelope, and read aloud as follows:

"MY OWN DEAR JACK—

"God grant you may never see these lines. Your mother loves you, Jacky, my boy; loves you, loves you. I am going to write something because I ought to, and not because I want to. I am getting old, and it won't be long before I go to meet him you used to call your daddy. My conscience is heavy, Jacky. My conscience makes me do this. I don't write it for you, I only write it because my conscience makes me. Don't think your old mother doesn't love you, boy. Don't think your daddy didn't. You know we did, and this minute, Jacky, you are sleeping where I hear you breathe; and this minute I kissed your forehead as you slept. Jacky, you are not my son. Don't be angry, dear. You are my own dear boy all the same, and I love you just the same. But you are not my son. We had a little fellow, too sweet to stay here long; and one day, these many, many years ago, your father brought you home. 'Here, dear,' said he, 'I've found another for you,' and you came right in my heart at once. He found you in the sewer, dear. He was out with his bag, and as he looked in the great hole at the foot of the City Hall Park, he heard a cry. He was a good man. He got you out. He brought you home. You cried for 'mamma,' and you called for 'papa,' but you were young, Jacky, dear, and such a pretty boy, I could not let you go. Next day, dear, we dressed you in our little Jacky's clothes, and tried to coax and question you. But it was all 'mamma' and 'papa' with you. Your clothes were spoiled, and you were sick. You only kept up a few hours, when fever set in. The doctor gave no hope, but I nursed you through, my boy, and in about a month you sat up straight in bed, for all the world like a beautiful star. But you knew nothing. We tried very hard, but could get nothing from you. I was sorry and glad. I wanted to keep you. We called you after my dead darling, and I hugged you in my arms for him. That's all, Jack, my boy. Let me call you Jack, my son. I shall do these clothes up in a bundle, and put this letter with 'em. You won't be likely to see it, Jack. If you don't, I shall be thankful. If you do, my boy, remember how your daddy loved you, and how your mother loves you, and forgive us if we have done wrong. Heaven preserve and protect you, Jack, my boy, my son, my darling.

"MOTHER."

"Forgive you?" said Hardy. "Forgive you?" Bless you, God bless you, you dear, honest, loving mother;" and he kissed the picture again and again.

"But who, then, am I?" said he. "Let's look at the clothes."

Nothing.

There was a little jacket with buttons all over it, and a jolly little pair of trowsers with a pocket on one side, and a make-believe pocket on the other.

But no mark of any kind.

Hardy's face was red with excitement.

Miller puffed quietly on.

A rap at the door, followed by Hardy's "come in," disclosed Mr. Russell, who looked at the two men and the disordered apartment in undisguised astonishment.

"Ah, come in, Mr. Russell, come in," said Hardy. "Excuse my lack of ceremony, and my excess of confusion. It doesn't look like me, I confess; but inasmuch as I don't know who I am, it matters very little. Sit down, please."

Mr. Russell was so taken aback by this unusual reception, that he hardly knew what to do.

He had always found Hardy respectful and considerate; now he found him brusque, and almost rude.

He looked at him closely, and seeing tears in the young man's eyes, pushed away the chair Miller had offered him, and laying his hand on Hardy's shoulder, said, as a father might to a son whom he loved: "Tell me, Hardy, what troubles you. Surely, I have the right to ask, and you know, my boy, that you have no right to conceal aught from me. Has Miller annoyed you?"

Miller looked up quickly, and said: "Mr. Russell, Mr. Hardy is your agent. We have buried the past between us. I have confessed my fault, and the truce is declared. I now ask your pardon, sir, and as I do so, let me couple my petition with a declaration of regard and esteem for this young man, for whom I would do anything in my power. No, sir, Miller has not annoyed him, but Miller will help him, and on that you may bet your bottom dollar."

Miller spoke slowly as was his habit, but he also spoke earnestly, and there was something so tender in his manner and expression, that Mr. Russell, whose heart was big and generous, extended his hand, and with a cordial grasp, said: "As you say, Mr. Miller; as you say. Bygones *shall* be bygones. Now tell me what under the sun is the matter with John Hardy?"

"Read this letter, sir," said Hardy; "that will tell you. I have lost my mother, sir; and my dear old father, too, who used to be so proud of his boy, is mine no longer. Oh, why did I open that infernal trunk?"

Mr. Russell read the letter through before he spoke. Then wiping his eyes, he turned to Hardy and said:

"Well, Hardy, this *is* rather rough. I know what it is to lose father and mother, by death. But I confess this is a touch beyond that. But those clothes. Is there nothing on them to indicate a clue?"

"Nothing, nothing at all," replied Hardy.

"Nothing but this," cried Miller, who had been turning the suit over and over; "nothing but this—."

Mr. Russell literally snatched the little jacket from the old man's hands.

On the loop, placed there for convenience of hanging the garment on a hook or nail, was a small sales ticket, on which was printed

"HALL, MILWAUKEE."

He could scarce believe his eyes.

"Hall, Milwaukee," cried he. "It cannot be. Oh, Hardy, speak, Miller, speak! Great heavens, can this be so! Hardy, Hardy, you are my son! I bought this suit myself. You wore it to New York when you were lost. Hardy! Hardy! For God's sake, help me, Miller. His foot! His foot!"

Quicker than a flash, old Miller pushed the half stupefied Hardy to a seat, drew off his gaiter, pulled off his sock—but no, they were all there!

"The other, man; the other. I told you the other," shouted Mr. Russell.

And there, sure enough, was the mutilated foot,

kissed by the father, shook by old Miller, and kissed and shook again, until in an ecstasy of joy, a perfect whirlwind of conflicting emotions, father and son held each other tight in a long and loving embrace.

Miller scratched his head.

"And now for home," said Mr. Russell; "how Maud's eyes will open, how—"

Maud!

Great heavens! Hardy had not thought of that, and burying his head in his pillow, he sobbed aloud.

Miller beckoned Mr. Russell to the window.

Placing his pipe on the sill, he took the astonished father by the hand.

"Mr. Russell, this is a matter of life or death, and you can alone decide it. Your son loves your daughter. He has found a father, but he loses a wife."

"Nonsense. Not at all, sir; not at all. Hardy, old fellow. Harry, my darling, look up! Dress yourself, and come with me. Your mother will want to see you. Aye, my boy, and your sweetheart will want to be the first to congratulate us both."

"What do you mean, sir?" said Hardy.

"What do I mean? Great Heaven, what do I *not* mean? Maud is not my child. Maud is not your sister. Her mother brought the dear girl with her when we were married. You shall wear her as you have won her, my son. *Now*, will you come?"

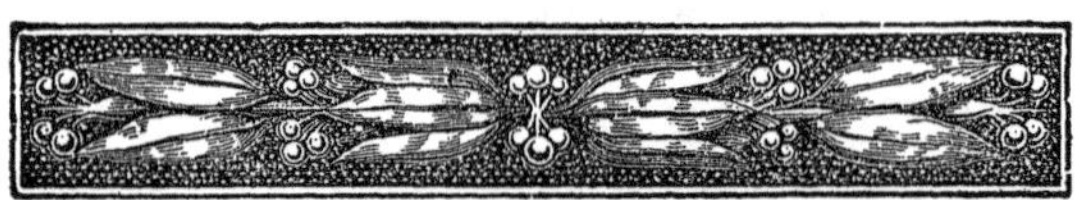

CHAPTER XXXIX.

THERE'S NO PLACE LIKE HOME.

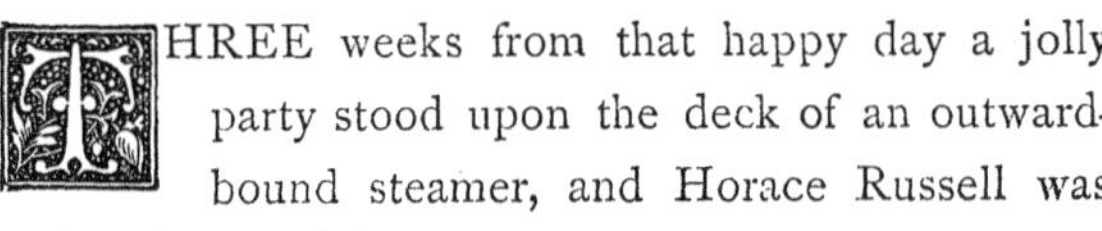

THREE weeks from that happy day a jolly party stood upon the deck of an outward-bound steamer, and Horace Russell was crying like a child.

Perhaps you think a strong man should not cry.

Well, let us see.

Just beyond him was a group, laughing, crying, shaking hands, and kissing:

Old Miller and Mary, Robert Delaney and Martha, John Hardy, or as he was then, Harry Russell, and Maud, his bride, with Mrs. Russell at their side.

Mr. Delaney and Martha were part of the travelling company, and Miller, with Mary, had come to bid them good-by.

Mr. Russell had arranged it all.

He had sent a check for $1,500 to the trustees of Mr. Delaney's church, with which to supply the pulpit for a year, and the young couple gladly availed themselves of the cordial invitation of their friend to pass that year abroad.

Maud had told her mother of Hardy's declaration, and they were discussing it, when Mr. Russell and his new found Harry made their appearance and disclosure.

Words cannot describe the scene that followed.

Suffice it that the lovers were married by the Rev. Robert Delaney, and that at the wedding breakfast the entire Miller family were honored guests.

" Home again," was now the cry of Horace Russell.

His affairs needed him?

Yes, but it was not for that he hurried.

He had found his son.

Twenty years' lost time must be made up.

The sooner he began the better.

With wife and son, and daughter, he craved his native air. He longed to present his boy, his son and heir to his workmen and his friends.

The future beckoned him with wide ambitions, in all of which John Hardy—Harry Russell—was an element.

How happy he was!

How happy they all were!

No wonder that the strong man wept.

THE END.

www.ingramcontent.com/pod-product-compliance
Lightning Source LLC
LaVergne TN
LVHW010218110826
845151LV00004B/1127
* 9 7 8 1 4 2 5 5 2 7 4 1 9 *